Gnashing Teeth Publishing
242 East Main Street
Norman AR 71960
http://GnashingTeethPublishing.com

Printed in the United States of America

ISBN 979-8-9898345-5-6

Fiction: Short Story Collection; Fiction: Short Stories

Gnashing Teeth Publishing First Edition

Their Foot Shall Slide in Due Time...and other stories

Zary Fekete

For Jasper Anderson

Table of Contents

Their Foot Shall Slide In Due Time 1

The Beast in the Hollow 19

Ramla Realizes 27

Alice and Roses 45

The Programmed Joy of Protection 57

Strawberry Skin 67

Lidérc 81

One Particular Girl on a Stage 91

Their Foot Shall Slide In Due Time

The wind was whipping through my thin slacks as I turned toward the last house on the street. The pants were not nearly thick enough for the weather, but Mr. Bishop insisted that this was the right uniform for piety: Black dress slacks and a white shirt beneath a black windbreaker which was issued to us by the company. On the windbreaker there was a small cross over the heart with the words "Bible Sales." Mr. Bishop said people should see me and think, *"I trust him. He is simple and honest. I want to buy his Bible."*

I felt the wheels of the pull-cart thunk into my Achilles tendon for what felt like the hundredth time. The cart was filled with dozens of copies of the Bible. Some were children's versions with lots of pictures. Some were bound in fake-leather with different colors. Some were larger with big type for people who were hard of seeing. They all started the day stacked neatly in my cart, but they always started to shift around when my route began each morning. I could never keep the books upright. No matter how I piled them they kept falling into a messy heap at the bottom of the fabric sack. The cart had a small handle for gripping. I kept switching my pulling hand so I could warm the other one in my pocket. Back and forth. Again and again. The temperature was fifteen degrees, but Mr. Bishop had things to say about that, too. In fact, he had a prayer for just such cold-weather moments. *"Oh, God, my God, in rain or shine. I am yours. You are mine."*

As I looked at the last house on the block I realized this one looked different. I should know. I had seen so many houses in the last four weeks. I approached them all in this same tentative way, ever since Father told me that he wanted me to do something to earn his generosity towards my college debt. In the fall I would be a freshman at the University of New Hampshire. I couldn't wait to get there, but it seemed light years away from that cold evening in my hometown of New Chastity.

I needed to try harder, I told myself. I needed to be more forthright. I needed to make some money. I've been all over this town. I started on the east side late November and now, here it was, almost Christmas. I had sold a grand total of two Bibles. And one was to my aunt.

This was not how I expected to spend the month of December. I thought I would be off with my friends, enjoying the lead up to the holidays, but Father had other plans. The Friday after Thanksgiving he called me into his study and laid out his plan.

"What kind of work?" I asked. Father didn't answer me right away. He leaned back in his study room chair and gazed along the rows and rows of Bibles and theological books behind him in the study. He tapped the spine of one of the thicker specimens and smiled.

He said he booked a job interview for me at the Increase Edmonds Bible Company. It was a relatively small printing press, but it had been in operation throughout the New England states since the Puritan Era. The Increase Edmonds Bible Company accounted for the majority of Bibles sold door to door, year after year, by ratio, throughout Vermont, Maine, Connecticut, and New Hampshire. Father said the sales success wasn't due to advertising or word of mouth. It was due to old-fashioned door knocking and persistence.

The orientation was held on a Saturday in the Bible Company headquarters, a drafty former schoolhouse on the edge of town. It was due to start at eight in the morning and was going to last into the evening. The instructions said to come promptly and to bring a notebook, a pencil, and a sack lunch.

About fifteen of us, all students, gathered into the room, blowing on our hands and shivering. We were there to meet Mr. Bishop, the main rep for the company. There was a wooden table against one of the walls. It was lined with a row of different kinds of Bibles, each published by the press. Some were big, weighing close to five pounds. Some were small pocket books. Some came with extra pages for taking notes. The Bibles all looked like the schoolhouse: old and cold.

After a moment, the door opened, letting in a blast of cold air. Mr. Bishop entered the room. He had a mane of white hair and big, bushy white eyebrows. He had no mustache but he had a beard, white like the rest of his hair. He was dressed in a severe black suit which was buttoned all the way up. He had no tie, but his white shirt beneath the suit jacket was also buttoned fast at his neck. He stood for a moment, surveying us, and then cleared his throat with a nod toward the school desks. We all took our seats and waited. Mr. Bishop walked to the front of the class and closed his eyes. A moment passed. The wind whistled somewhere above us in the attic.

"I will begin with a prayer," he said. His voice was pinched and reedy. We all bowed our heads. There was silence for a moment. Then Mr. Bishop said, "Sweet Lord. Guide our time and our minds. Fill us with your Holy Spirit. Send these young arms, laden with your Word, into your fields ripe for planting. Amen." A few of the students muttered "amen." We looked up.

"Well, dear friends," he said, looking at us each in turn. "By coming here today you are demonstrating something to me. You are showing me that you are interested in the business of the good news. You are among a special group. You are the thirty-fifth orientation class I have instructed. I do this once a year. I was once sitting…" he paused and pointed to the front desk with a faint glow of pride in his eyes, "right there. And on that day my father was the instructor. He was with the Bible Company since the first decade of the twentieth century. He died last year. He died," Mr. Bishop gestured into the air, "in this very room."

The students near the back of the room looked at each other with raised eyebrows. Mr. Bishop didn't notice. He was already onto the next thought.

"He died of a heart attack. He was in this very room, preparing for last year's orientation. My father was devoted," Mr. Bishop said. "He was a strict father, but a faithful Bible salesman. During the years he worked for the company he traveled across half of the state more than fifty times. He calculated he must have visited every house in all twenty counties at least five times over the course of his life. He experienced all kinds of sales attempts. Some people bought a Bible. Some people did not. Not all sales attempts went well. He was sometimes chased by dogs. One man struck my father in the mouth with a thrown baseball. Two of my father's teeth were knocked out. He went back to the same house a year later. When the same man opened the door, my father said, 'God seeks you, good man.' That man bought a Bible that day."

A silence settled over the classroom. The ticking of the stove's heat filled the quiet between Mr. Bishop's sentences.

"The Reverend Increase Edmonds founded this Bible Sales company. He did so in the eighteenth century as the mayor of New Chastity. There he is." Mr. Bishop gestured to a painted portrait on the wall. The man in the picture had green eyes and a severe mouth. He had white hair. He wore a black suit, buttoned to the neck like Mr. Bishop's. His left hand held a Bible. His right hand was pointing up at the sky.

"There was a strict code of morality for the town," Mr. Bishop said. "Edmonds required the town to rise before dawn for communal prayers. The town gathered into the main square, right in front of the church, all year. The prayers were required regardless of the weather. One winter the temperature reached thirty-five degrees below zero. Edmonds was waiting, knee deep in snow in the town center. When Edmonds heard that five families had stayed at home that day, he excommunicated them from the church and they were banished from the township. That was in the country's early days. There was no world outside of the town. All five families died that winter in the forests surrounding the town where they tried to find shelter. When Edmonds heard this, he called the town together for a special meeting. 'I am sad for their souls,' he said to the crowd. 'But I am not sad for our loss. God wants commitment. Not contentment.'"

As Mr. Bishop spoke, he began to pace back and forth in front of the class, occasionally touching the row of Bibles or gesturing at Edmonds portrait. "He was hard on lawbreakers and punished them himself," Mr. Bishop said. "One day, after church, several of the teenage boys got ahold of a medical journal with pictures of the male and female anatomy drawn in fine pencil lines. They smuggled it with them into school the next day and were giggling through its pages when Edwards heard about what was happening. He brought the boys out into the town square and searched them. When he found the journal, he called all the townspeople to the square. Edwards performed the whipping himself. The eyewitnesses said as they saw each crack of the whip come down on the backs of the boys, Edwards' eyes flashed and spittle ran from his mouth with the effort. As he whipped he rhythmically repeated the words, *'No gods but God!'* The witnesses said he didn't stop whipping until the boys were hoarse with cries and the blood was dripping into pools on the ground below."

After these words, Mr. Bishop stopped and looked at us for a long moment. Then he turned and looked again at the portrait of Edwards on the blackboard. I looked around the room. Several students were staring at him with their mouths open. That was just before noon. When lunch break was over most of the students had bowed out. There were only four of us left.

That afternoon Mr. Edwards drilled the four of us repeatedly with phrases that he said would guarantee us sale upon sale throughout the month of December. He asked us to repeat the phrases after him:

"A Bible soothes an angry word and calms an anxious heart.

From God's lips to thine ears.

Little flock, gentle flock, where ever you look, you'll find every problem solved in the Good Book."

There were several other lines as well. Some of them were Bible verses. One was just the chanting repetition of the word "Glory…glory…glory."

We repeated the lines, even the ones that we didn't really understand. Mr. Bishop made us promise that we would continue to repeat them and recite them to ourselves after the orientation was over. We were eager to get going.

At the end of the day, Mr. Bishop asked us to line up in front of the Bible table. He held a large tattered copy in his hands, his own Bible. One by one, we placed our right hand on the black book and said the words, "God's Word. My task. His flock. Amen." Then we received our black pants, white shirt, and windbreaker.

We were released, each of us clutching a personalized list of addresses. The town was marked out carefully on a map. Each us received our own folded paper copy of the map. There was also a large map tacked to the back wall next to the cross. Before I left that day, I looked at my section of the city, passing my eye along the rows and rows of streets, visualizing the houses one after another, imagining the money.

The first week was miserable. I started in the blue-collar section of the town. Most people weren't home. The folks who were at home were mostly polite, but they didn't want Bibles. One guy met me at the door with a half-full bottle of Jack Daniels. He was wearing ripped blue jeans and no shirt. When I showed him my pull cart of Bibles he tapped the bottle with his finger. "My Bible," he said. Then he closed the door in my face.

I didn't want the misery of the first week to discourage me. It must get better, I thought. People must buy Bibles from time to time. Otherwise how would the company stay in business? I tried to picture Increase Edmonds as I went from door to door. I had his portrait in my mind. He imagined him, three hundred years ago, walking through these same streets. Mr. Bishop had given us a thorough image of the man.

Edmonds would preach on Sundays for two to three hours, completely without notes. He started from one simple Bible passage and then slowly unfolded a rippling sermon filled with cries for repentance and admonishment for sins.

His most famous sermon had become legendary and notorious among the early Puritan writings. It was entitled *Their Foot Shall Slide in Due Time*. It was the first true catalyst for the Great Awakening which spread throughout the New England area in the 1700s.

He preached the sermon on July 8th, 1741, in the heat of the summer. The church was already warm from the morning sunshine. By the time the parishioners had gathered in the pews the historians believe the temperature in the wooden building was higher than 90 degrees. People were dressed, head to toe, in their black Sunday best. I tried to imagine this as I walked through the snowy streets of New Chastity with my Bible cart.

Edmonds began the sermon by slowly unfolding his grievances with the town. He remembered peoples' trespasses by name. He pointed, one by one, to different people in the audience, asking them, "You, sir. You, madam. Will your foot slide? When God opens the ground beneath you in the final hour, will your grip hold?" As he pointed around the sanctuary the gazes fell before his firm look. He held his hand out over the congregation, asking them to picture his hand as God's hand, held aloft and hovering, held in check by God's will, held, but ever able to drop in a strike of judgment.

He spoke on, his volume rising as he warmed to the subject, "The only reason your foot has not slipped is because he has not willed it. He restrains his strike for his pleasure. You deserve his blow. Were you to see yourselves aright, you should lift your faces and ask for his chastening strike."

The congregation began to fidget. Eyewitnesses later said a spell seemed to be hovering over the room. They were all, to a person, moved to feel intense spiritual conviction. The audience members said they felt their lives passing through their minds, their deepest, most private moments, exposed as though the entire world could see them.

Edmonds continued to hold his hand out over the crowd. He said, "In God's hand you are as flies, pinched between his fingers. He could, in a moment, crush you. It is his supreme will which withholds his wrath. He dangles you over a flame, allowing the singing of your black wings."

Women in the audience removed their black kerchiefs and began to pull them back and forth across their necks, burning their skin from the friction. Men begin to dig at their arms with their nails, drawing deep furrows of blood across their wrists.

Edmonds voice cracked from exertion as he spoke on. "The devil is ready to fall upon you. You are his goods, his property. Without God you have no security against him."

By the time the sermon ended, three hours later, the temperature in the church was close to 105 degrees. Women had fainted. Men were tearing their clothes. Children were scattered this way and that, some trying to imitate their parents' confessions, while others just sat in the pews sobbing and begging to leave.

Mr. Bishop had told us this history with a grave expression. He said he was not sensationalizing the information. He used it as a way to bolster our confidence. He wanted us to carry forth this word of judgment to the people across New Chastity as Edmonds had done hundreds of years ago. I thought about this as I trekked through the snowy streets. I continued to knock on each door, but I kept being turned away. With each door that closed in my face I felt Mr. Bishop's frowning eyes looking down on me. I wondered what he would say when I returned at the end of the season with just a few Bibles sold.

From the blue-collar section I moved through the downtown area. This was a section of mostly businesses and townhouses. The businesses all had strict rules against solicitation. I tried at the barber shop and the owner just shook his head. The townhouses all had housewives with their hair in buns. Some of them smiled and shook their heads. One lady told me she was Jewish.

Over the course of the next few weeks I slowly made may way street by street. I had plenty of time to stew in my own thoughts. I was nervous about disappointing Mr. Bishop, but I was terrified of returning to my father with nothing to show for my efforts.

There was a reason my father was so excited for me to work for the Edmonds Bible Company. My parents were strict Christians. We attended the main church in town, the same one Edmonds founded. It was housed in a new building now, but it was still on the main block of the town. All the other business radiated out from it. Even people who didn't go to church probably passed the huge stained-glass windows of the church as they went about their daily business.

As I made my way through the business district, getting one rejection after another, I thought about my parents. I also thought about Increase Edwards, whipping the boys in the town square.

Near the end of our orientation day, Mr. Bishop told us a final story about Edmonds. He told us to remember it before we began to make the sales rounds. It played through my mind the next afternoon while my mother was ironing my black pants and white shirt. I had not been able to stop thinking about it.

After the famous, inflammatory sermon, Edmonds began to journey into the surrounding countryside on his first few Bible sales attempts. He had a horse-drawn wagon, filled with Bibles, and people from the surrounding farms said they knew he was coming when they saw a cloud of dust rising up from the dirt road, like some kind of sandstorm of impending judgment.

Edmonds trained a group of young men as disciples who he intended to send into the surrounding counties to sell Bibles. He planned a special orientation ceremony for them one night. He brought the men into a small grove of woods next to the lake, just outside of the town. One of the men wrote an account of the training which was later published in the Journal of Puritan Era Witchcraft History.

Edmonds built a fire and stacked the Bibles around it in small piles. He assigned each man one of the piles to guard. The men were confused. Edmonds said wherever the word of God was preached there would be those who received it and those who refused.

Edmonds began to stir the flames of the bonfire. He opened his Bible and began to read, "Thou shalt not suffer a witch to live. They shall be stoned."

He looked up from the Bible and gestured toward the dark woods to his side. Two of the constables of the village who were waiting in the shadows came forward. They held a woman between them bound in chains.

"Bring her forward," Edmonds said. The constables brought the woman to the edge of the fire.

"Gentlemen," he said to the young men around the fire. "Take up the sword of the spirit." He grabbed one of the Bibles from the pile in front of him and held it into the air. The young men were confused. None of them moved.

"Take it up!" he said. "What are thee? Boys? Take it. Make it thy hand." He circled around behind them, prodding them with the book he held. Slowly, nervously, each young man took a book from the piles in front of them.

"Now," Edmonds said. "You see this one?" He pointed to the bound girl. "She is unchecked. Lawless." He walked up to her. "Given free reign she would draw others. She loves not God. She loves the darkness. Suffer her not." He drew his arm back and threw the book at the bound woman. It struck her on the forehead, causing her to stagger backwards. The hem of her dress caught aflame. The fire raced up her skirts. Shadows of the flames flickered across the faces of the young men who looked at the girl with gaping mouths.

"The devil has her now," Edmonds cried out. "Expose the sin below! Fan the refiner's fire." Foam flew from his lips. The woman was screaming as the flames consumed her. Some of the men turned aside. One of them vomited.

Edmonds began to shriek, racing back and forth between them, striking them with his hands and slapping their faces. He screamed at them. Then he lifted his leg and kicked the woman full into the fire. Instantly she was ablaze. She screamed and raked her face with her fingernails in agony. She tried to come out of the fire.

"See!" he said. "See how she attempts to circumvent her sin! But God spies her. He will not be denied her judgment. Throw, men of God!"

The men later said they don't remember who threw the first book, but the dam broke, and the air was filled with flying, hurtling Bibles. Most of them struck her torso, but one hit her eye. The eyeball, already smoking from the fire, burst and ran down her face. Soon the woman was on her knees. Her screams died down until all she did was bubble and chatter her teeth together in the agony of death. The Bibles, one by one, caught on fire and added to the height of the flames. The night sky above was filled with swirling cinders.

At least ten other young women died in New Chastity in the following months. After Mr. Bishop told us this story in class, he solemnly turned to the row of Bibles standing on the table behind him.

"Increase Edmonds was a man of his time," Mr. Bishop said. "He was fallible. But there is no denying he loved God and guarded his word jealously." He picked up a Bible from the table and held it out toward us with both of his hands. "Remember. You are selling more that Bibles. You are selling the path of salvation."

Mr. Bishop's words echoed in my head as I turned onto the last street. I had knocked on all the doors except this last house, the final one on the block.

As I walked toward this last house, I glanced at my paper map. Strange. This house wasn't on the map. The map only showed an empty field. I felt the whip of the wind again, so I shrugged and put the map away. I repeated the phrase in my head that I had been reciting throughout the morning: *I will sell these Bibles today.* In addition to the phrases, Mr. Bishop encouraged us to repeat Bible verses to ourselves. I couldn't quite remember which verse he suggested. Something about "meek", but I couldn't remember. So instead I had my own little phrase. I repeated again, *I will sell these…*

I lifted the pushcart over the small lip of the driveway which led up to the house. The driveway felt a little longer than the other ones. The house seemed to be huddled against itself on the outskirts of the neighborhood. It looked old. It was made of old-fashioned wooden planks. There was a curl of smoke coming out of the chimney. I didn't see any lights on…no, wait. There was a faint glow from one of the windows. I walked up to the front door and looked for the doorbell. There wasn't one. Instead, there was a door knocker. It was a heavy brass affair which looked like it weighed several pounds.

I lifted it and knocked twice. I waited. *I will sell…*

I heard the sound of a faucet or something turning off inside the house. Then there were footsteps approaching. A light went on in the hallway. The door opened.

It was a lady. She was old, in her seventies. She was wearing a heavy knit green sweater. Her hair was in a tight bun, a mix of grey and white. She had a pair of reading glasses hanging on a string of beads around her neck. Her eyes were very green.

"Yes?" she smiled.

I took a breath and started, "Good aft… I mean, good evening, ma'am. Sorry to bother you, but could I ask you a question?"

I felt her eyes flick me up and down as she sized me up. I prepared myself for the standard answer…but she surprised me.

"Of course, sir," she said. "Why don't you come in?"

For a moment I didn't move. I had never gotten that far before. I remembered Mr. Bishop's words, *"If they invite you in, they have already decided they want to buy one."* I carefully lifted the pushcart over the threshold. The front hallway was warm, uncomfortably so. A moment ago, I was freezing, but now I felt a drop of sweat forming under my armpit.

"Thank you, ma'am."

She had already turned away from the door and was walking down the short hallway toward the kitchen.

I took one Bible out of the pushcart and followed her. My palm was wet with sweat and I could feel the brown faux-leather of the book grow slippery. I could feel the drop of sweat from my armpit start to slide its long journey down toward my waist. She was waiting for me when I reached the kitchen. Without asking me whether I wanted one, she placed a cup of steaming tea on the table, "Sit. Cold out there."

"Yes, a little," I said. I sat and took a sip as I glanced around the room. It was very clean. I smelled dish soap and coffee.

She sat down opposite me. Her green eyes were soft but alert. "Now then. You had a question for me?"

I blinked a couple of times. Something felt off, but I couldn't tell what it was. "Uh. Yes, well." For a moment my words trailed off but then I imagined Mr. Bishop's firm glance, and I cleared my throat. "Yes, ma'am. What if I told you I had something that could change your life?"

She was looking at me very intently. After a small pause she said, "Well, that certainly sounds like something, right?"

I swallowed, marveling at my good luck, and continued, "Yes, that's right, ma'am. And I'm not here to waste anyone's time. Do you know what is the best-selling book in the world?"

She continued her steady gaze. She hadn't blinked once yet. She said, "I've got a guess, but I'll let you tell me."

I gave a practiced smile and held up the Bible with a little flourish. "Here she is," I said. "Now I know you hear all sorts of talk these days about religion being a waste of time. But, let me set the news straight." I tapped the cover. "This book. This is no ordinary book. This book has traveled through time to meet you here today."

She held my eyes for a moment, then dropped her eyes to the book in my hand. I could feel another drop of sweat readying itself in my armpit. I tried to keep my hand firm.

She looked back up at me. "Sir," she said. "Tell me more."

The second drop of sweat started to roll. I twisted my body slightly, trying to catch the sweat with my shirt. I couldn't believe I'd gotten this far. In fact, I didn't know what else to say.

"Well," I said. "There's… what you need to understand is that this book…"

She held up her finger and stopped me mid-sentence. My tongue was curled against the roof of my mouth. She kept her finger up and her eyes sized me up again, like she was trying to decide what kind of words to choose.

"Sir," she said, and then she paused. When she continued to speak her voice was even and steady, almost salesman-like. "Sir, you were doing fine. You were building up a nice head of steam. In fact, you sounded sure. You were talking about that book like it was part of you." She paused and frowned slightly. "But when the time came to close in and show me the full truth, I believe you dried up."

I felt a bit slighted. "Now, ma'am, let me…" But she stopped me with a wave of her finger.

"Hold on, now," she said. "You've already had some time, and now I want to see where things stand. Sir, I can tell you want to sell me this book. And I can tell you've thought a lot about how it would feel to get a sale. I suspect there are people who sent you, and they might have told you what to expect. Am I right about some of that?"

I waited, uncertain whether I should answer her. My grip on the faux-leather Bible slipped a bit and it dangled in my fingers. A new drop of sweat formed on my temple.

She continued, "I think that's right. I think you spent time with others who gave you certain words to say. They might have told you some things about the history of that book and about what hands have gripped it through time. How those words have stirred kings and armies and laid enemies low. I imagine they filled your head with thoughts of glory and sales and righteous steps towards God's kingdom. Am I on the right path?"

The Bible fell out of my hand and landed with a crisp thud on the table. My tea cup rattled and a drop of hot liquid leapt out onto my wrist. I flinched slightly. I suddenly realized I desperately wanted to leave. I didn't want to be in that hot kitchen anymore. I quickly picked up the Bible and made a gesture to stand up. But she put up her hand and plowed on forward.

"Yes, I'm quite sure I've got some of that right," she said. "And from the heft of that pull-cart back there and the effort you took to hitch it up into my hallway, I suspect it's still full of books. And I think that's not just true for today. I think you may have been at this task for the last few weeks and that you may not have sold much yet. In fact, I think maybe you haven't sold even one. Is that how it is?"

My mouth closed and opened silently. I cleared my throat again. "Now, that's not true," I managed to say, "And, I just started this month, so things will..."

She interrupted me again, "That's alright, and no shame to it. Every day is a long river, and the night comes sooner every evening. The farmer plows the rows and fertilizes the field, but then there's the long, cold winter before the crop." She said all this with a practiced riff, like she was a carnival barker selling three balls to try to knock down milk jugs at the state fair.

In the silence that followed I heard a clock ticking from the other room. The wind outside gave a quick burst and a high whine came through a gap under one of her window sills. I looked down the front hallway, desperate to leave.

She said, "So, it comes back to the first point I made. I know you've been told some people buy Bibles and some don't. I know that once this county was barren as the sea bed with heathen and sinners. And I know New Chastity has a special place in God's eye because of the efforts of young men like you since the whole enterprise began. And, of course, we're not just talking about the Sales Company. We're talking about when God spoke the words before they were put into a book. And now, through God's grace, there *is* a bound book of truth and promises. A book that can and must be offered to the unchurched masses. So, it comes back to the first point: I can tell that you want to sell me this book. But I'm not sure whether you are convinced that you *must* sell it to me. Do you see that?"

No one had ever said this much to me before. Mr. Bishop had nothing for this. I didn't know what to think. I said, "Well, ma'am, that's not how I see it. I am just here offering you a..."

She stood abruptly. My words cut out like a light being flicked off. She looked at me with a long, even stare. Then she took a step closer to me.

"Sir," she said. "May I show you something?"

I didn't know what to say. My tongue felt frozen.

"Come with me," she said. Against my will, I stood. She walked back down the short front hallway. There was a door I hadn't noticed when I came it. She opened it. Behind it was a set of steps leading down to the cellar. "This way," she said and walked down before me.

I glanced at the front door. I wanted to leave. But somehow, I didn't. I felt caught between fear and a still-alive desire for a successful sale. I took a breath and followed her down the stairs.

It was dark in the cellar. There was a snap, and I realized she had pulled one of those old-fashioned light bulb strings. A single light came alive and threw weak rays of electric light around the basement. The loose swinging of the light bulb caused shadows to move back and forth on the walls.

She moved toward the back wall of the cellar, and as I followed her, I saw a picture on the wall slowly come into view in the dusty air. I couldn't quite make it out. I walked a bit closer and then, with a silent gasp, I saw who it is. It was the severe face of Increase Edmonds looking out at me. In the dim, shadowed light, the paint which formed his green eyes seemed to glisten. It looked remarkably lifelike. His eyes seemed to follow me. I felt a thin sheen of goosebumps raise up on my arms.

The lady stood next to the portrait, looking at it with quiet reverence. Then she turned back to me. For a moment, I thought I was imagining things. Was that...?

"Sir," she said. "Did Mr. Bishop tell you the story of Edmond's last Bible campaign?"

I shook my head. I almost missed the fact that she knew Mr. Bishop's name. I hadn't mentioned him to her. How?

She continued, "It was a cold one. The winter of 1741. The historians said the December temperature hovered near zero all through the month. Water in the wells froze right through. The ice had to be chipped free and melted on the stove before anyone could take a drink."

As she talked she looked back at the portrait. She took one of her fingers and traced it along the bottom of the frame. "Yes, it was cold. That season Mr. Edmonds trained a group of young people, the same way he always did. He sat them down in his classroom and told them the story of the Gospel. But that year Mr. Edmonds allowed one change. Up until then he only taught young men. He didn't much trust women. Thought they were flighty and wayward. But that year was different. He had a baby sister. She came of age that year. She had turned 18. He made an exception for her. He let her enter the class of hopeful Bible sellers."

She continued to talk. Her tracing finger moved up from the frame of the portrait and she began to gently stroke Edmonds' white hair. "He was tough on her. He was always tough, but he held out some exceptions for her. She had to memorize long parts of the scripture. He quizzed her. Held a cane while he did it. If she got so much as a word off he rapped her knuckles. Kept it up until her hands with raw and bloody. But she stayed with it and soon she had the whole New Testament memorized.

"When the time came he sent the boys into the surrounding county like he always did. But he had something special planned for the girl. He sent her into the woods. That's where the outcasts were sent. People who lived in the woods were cold and cruel. That's where he sent her."

She stopped. She was looking up at the portrait. She held her gaze firm. There was a long pause.

"What happened?" I said.

She looked back at me. "No one knows, because she never came back."

I stammered for a moment. "She died?" I said.

"Some say she froze. Some say the castaways cut her up. Some say she's out there still. This town hasn't changed that much. The woods to the north are still a bit rough. A good place for a ghost to dwell." The lady stopped looking at the portrait and looked back at me. Her green eyes were sharp. "Or maybe she has her own house now."

The wind outside gave off a loud howl. The hair on the back of my neck was standing up. I felt my skin rippling with goosebumps. She kept staring at me. Then she took a step forward. Her mouth quivered into a weird smile. I backed up. She kept coming toward me. I turned quickly and scrambled up the steps, taking them two by two. I expected to feel her hand close around my ankle any second. Then I was back in the front hallway. I ran to the front door and flung it open. I took a huge leap and landed on the driveway, running toward the street.

"Sir," I heard her voice. It sounded like she was right next to me. She was speaking quietly, but I could hear her, even through the wind. The voice was firm enough to make me stop. I turned around slowly. She was standing in the doorway, holding the handle of my pull cart.

I quickly walked back up, grabbed the handle, and backed away again.

"Thank you, ma'am," I said.

Her gaze didn't falter. Then she slowly reached down and pushed up the sleeve of her green sweater. She had the old, wrinkled skin of the elderly, but something was different about her arm. I stared at it. The entire arm was white. Not just pale. It was absolutely snow white. And there were patches of ice on it.

She said, "I've been around for a while, son. I've watched this neighborhood change. This used to all be all prairie and woods. But 300 years is a long time and even the curve of the land will change if you give it enough rope."

She smiled. I noticed her eyes again, so green. I realized I was still holding the Bible in my hand. It was dangling limply between my fingers. The wind caught some pages and the cover blew open. I looked down. I could see the title page, flickering in the wind. I saw the words *Holy Bible,* and below that I saw the imprint "Increase Edmonds Bible Company." Every Bible the company sold started with that page. And below the words was a portrait of Edmonds, stamped on the front page.

With slow horror I looked down and saw Increase Edmonds' picture looking up at me, his green eyes were piercing and sharp. I looked back at her. Her green eyes glowed. She stepped toward me. She smiled. She had no teeth. Her mouth was a black crack. The resemblance was uncanny.

She had almost reached me. I wanted to run, but I couldn't. She stopped in front of me and held up a white hand, pointing at the sky.

"It takes faith to sell Bibles, son," she said slowly. "Faith…and blood." She smiled wider and her gums stretched beneath her lips. A blast of wind cut between us and I staggered back a step.

She turned to go back inside, but stopped. She turned back. Her smile was gone. "When you're ready," she said, "knock again."

The Beast in the Hollow

Some say it's a trick of the light. Others claim it is because of the size of the three canvases. What is clear is when you enter the Munkácsy Gallery you feel a sense of vertigo.

I remember my first trip to the museum. I was eleven. It was for a fifth-grade field trip from my primary school in Budapest. Our teachers planned cultural events like this quite often. By the time I was ten years old I had already attended, with my class of twenty-five other precocious students, three operas, five ballets, and dozens of trips to museums throughout our country. Many of those experiences were unmemorable. But I will never forget the Munkácsy Gallery.

It was bright autumn with the leaves just beginning to change. We took the train two hours east of Budapest to the provincial town of Debrecen. Our little class was bubbling with excitement, much to the consternation of our teachers. Our enthusiasm gave rise to paper airplane throwing contests up and down the train carriage and countless smeared fingerprints on every inch of the windows as we pointed out to one another the cows in the pastures, the leaves falling in the forests, and the many bicyclers wobbling their way through the shabby countryside of Hungary during the waning years of the Socialist 1980s. By the time the train pulled into Debrecen, the country town which was home to the Deri Museum where the Munkácsy Gallery was housed, our teachers had impressed upon us a need to behave in a decorous manner.

The museum was a short fifteen-minute walk from the train station, and we all held hands with our partners and walked in a careful line behind the teacher. Our clean school uniforms caught the eyes of many passersby who must have recalled similar school expeditions from their own young years. We finally reached the museum and made our way up the central path between well-trimmed hedges.

No sooner had we entered the museum than the sunlight was shut out with the closing of a massive wooden door and a tall, elderly museum director stood before us. He seemed, to my young eyes, impossibly old, with creases and wrinkles spiderwebbing their way across his gaunt face. He said nothing, yet his daunting presence caused all of us to lose our inclination towards chatter and we followed him silently through several dim hallways until we finally came to a halt outside the entry to the Munkácsy Gallery.

It was here that our guide finally introduced himself. He turned and spoke to us in a low voice which held within it a tone of effortless gravity, as though the owner of the voice knew, merely by speaking, that our class would be held in rapt attention, as indeed we were.

He introduced himself as Mr. Bocskai. He had, as we soon learned, been the museum director for the last thirty years, but the Munkácsy paintings preceded him by one and a half centuries. They were painted in the middle of the 1800s by Munkácsy Mihály, a painter whose name any Hungarian grade school student would recognize, even if they did not precisely know why.

Mr. Bocskai explained to us, in ever deeper tones, the snapshot history of the paintings. Munkácsy painted the three canvases during a period near the end of his life when most historians believed he had succumbed to insanity. Up until the two-year period when he completed the three paintings, he had been most well-known for his work chronicling the daily lives of Hungarian peasants. He underwent, however, a religious conversion after the death of his mother in 1856, after which he spent a complete three months confined to his bedroom in his family estate in eastern Hungary. Few details were known about those three months except he was attended to by a single manservant who brought him regular food and drink. This man would claim, on his own deathbed, that the room in which Munkácsy lived during those three months had been painted completely black and that Munkácsy not only did no painting during that span of time but also kept with him nothing but a small journal in which he recorded his thoughts. The manservant reported that on many a night during those three months he could hear, emanating from the bedchamber, not only Munkácsy's voice, lamenting the loss of his mother, but the voice of a second person. Munkácsy spoke questions and the manservant heard the voice give answers, but it spoke not in Hungarian but in an indecipherable foreign tongue. The manservant said this second voice had no identifiable pitch, but warbled both high and low and never failed to send a shudder of fear through him when he heard it.

When Munkácsy emerged from his room after his three-month self-imposed silence, he stripped his portrait studio of all previous works and began immediately upon the three canvases which became his most famous works. Munkácsy completed the final painting on a Saturday and promptly shut himself into his attic and hung himself. He was found three days later by his manservant. There was no suicide note. There was only a single piece of paper on which was scrawled, "The beast in the shadow will not leave."

Mr. Bocskai stopped speaking. A chill ran through my veins. When he spoke again it was to tell us the rules we were to follow when we entered the gallery. We were, he impressed upon us, not to touch the paintings—in fact we were advised to stand in the center of the gallery, at least five feet away from the canvases. The paint was ancient and had, for the sake of authenticity, not been treated with any preserving chemicals. The air in the gallery was filtered from the center of the room directly up into a series of pipes. These carried all olfactory evidence of human visitors so that nothing, not even a tiny smear of human skin oil in the air, could mar the surface of the three paintings.

We were not allowed to take any photographs of the paintings. There was no food or drink allowed in the chamber. We were not permitted to speak in any voice above that of a whisper for fear that the air in the room might be disturbed in the slightest way and which might thus inadvertently cause some minute damage to the paint or canvas surface.

And finally, Mr. Bocskai maintained, with utter conviction, while we *were* allowed to look at the three paintings, there was one *particular* spot we must avoid looking at. It was at this point that Mr. Bocskai stopped speaking and took several deep breaths, as though he was composing himself. We, as a class, collectively held our breath and leaned closer to him in the silence.

When he spoke again, he described to us the reason for the caution. Mr. Bocskai told us that the paintings were of three particular moments from the life of Christ. The first was *Golgota*, a picture of the crucified Jesus on the hill. The second was *Christ Before Pilate*, which was a visual representation of the Messiah presented to the Roman magistrate. The third, and when he spoke of it his voice diminished to a whisper, was the dangerous painting in question. It was called *Ecce Homo*, a visual portrayal of Pilate presenting Jesus to the crowd.

Mr. Bocskai said all three pictures were masteries in form. They each were immensely large, covering the three walls of the gallery in which they hung. The centerpiece of each picture was, obviously, the character of Jesus, but gathered around the Christ in each picture were all manner of smaller descriptive visual moments. The pictures were filled with figures of people in various poses, and each smaller moment in the larger picture was meant to tell a portion of a greater story. In one corner of *Christ Before Pilate*, men argued over Jesus's condemnation. There were, in a distant section of *Golgota*, tearful women, hands thrown to the air, despairing over Christ's death. Mr. Bocskai described the paintings, in a manner designed undoubtedly to appeal to our young crowd, as though he were referencing a nineteenth-century version of a comic book in which many small, individual pictures made up the entirety of the complete work of art.

Ordinarily this news would have elicited a series of playful comments from me and my friends, but we were still spellbound and gripped with a desire to know the darker secret. We still had not heard the mystery of the dangerous spot in the third painting. Finally, he bent forward to unfold the final secret.

Mr. Bocskai said it was the third painting, *Ecce Homo*, which was the most controversial. In the picture, Pilate stands on a raised balcony and presents Jesus to a crowd, impelling them to free him rather than condemn him to death. Jesus himself stands with his eyes heavenward, calmly accepting whatever fate might come; indeed, knowing what the outcome will be. The crowd below Pilate alternately fumes with desire for the crucifixion and shivers with hope that the sentence will be averted.

Mr. Bocskai took out a handkerchief to mop his brow and then said, "And now, children, the moment which I must insist upon receiving your greatest attention." And indeed, he had it, for we were rapt in the telling of his tale. He told us of the mysterious spot. It was located upon the section of canvas directly behind Pilate's head. He said we would know it immediately because it was a darker spot of paint, comprised mostly of dark browns and blacks, as though that section of the ancient scene was meant to evoke shadows and a hollow from the sun. Mr. Bocskai said it was in this dark section behind Pilate's head where, if one's gaze lingered too long, one would see the faintest impression of a shape. It was the shape of a demon. Because of the suicide, Munkácsy was never able to tell his side of the story. But many art historians believed this dark figure, hovering behind the head of Pilate, was intended, by Munkácsy, to represent a dark force which compelled Pilate to finally sentence Jesus to his death.

When Mr. Bocskai revealed this to us, a small shudder touched my frame. I thought, in my mind's eye, I could see this dark figure, though I had never before seen the painting. I imagined it, hovering behind Pilate's head. I imagined I could see faint yellow hollows, eyes in the dark paint. Near the back of our crowd, one of my classmates began to cry, and a teacher immediately swooped in to comfort her. The rest of us, still completely spellbound, continued to lean forward, hoping against our better judgment to hear more.

Mr. Bocskai said the story of the demon in the canvas slowly grew over time. Once the canvases were completed, they were initially taken on a tour throughout Europe and the United States. Little evidence of trouble presented itself from the first smattering of viewings. It wasn't until a wealthy American department store magnate, John Wanamaker, purchased the paintings that the tale turned. Wanamaker conceived of an idea for the paintings to be displayed annually in the week leading up to Easter, as was befitting of the canvases' Biblical theme. Wanamaker decreed the paintings were to be displayed in the Grand Court of his Philadelphia department store, but the installation of the paintings proved troublesome. Their size was more immense than anything previously hung in the store, and the fragile nature of the canvases required greater reinforcement before they could be hung. The services of a portrait hanger were secured, a man named Bartholomew Stringer. Stringer spent a day surveying the Grand Court of the Philadelphia store and then resolved to examine the paintings individually once the store had closed for the evening.

The next day when the store was opened, Stringer was found dead on the floor before *Ecce Homo*, his body rigid in a seated position. A doctor was called for who promptly examined Stringer's body and determined the cause of death to be a heart attack brought upon by shock.

Stringer was given a proper Christian funeral in his home church north of Philadelphia. Unusually, the church was required to hold a closed casket ceremony. The reason being that Stringer's eyes could not be closed. Each time the lids were pressed into a likeness of sleep, they popped open again in a sprightly yet gruesome display of alertness. The funeral director maintained he could not send anyone on their journey into the beyond while their eyes still hungered for some purchase on the land of the living.

A private investigator was hired to look into the manner of Stringer's death, and he found nothing of suspicion, save a single piece of paper upon which was scrawled, in Stringer's handwriting, a single crooked sentence. The sentence read, "The beast in the hollow beckons me."

Several other of my classmates were whimpering and sobbing by this point, and the teachers were pulling brave duty, soothing the troubled spirits which were manifest all around our sorry group. I felt a tug of conscience, wondering whether I might be of use to my teachers, yet I could not pull myself away from the tale which Mr. Bocskai had not quite concluded.

After he composed himself, Mr. Bocskai spoke again. After the Philadelphia ordeal, Wanamaker tired of the controversy which inevitably swirled around the gathering stories regarding the painting's Biblical curse. He sold the canvases to the national museum in Prague where a number of prominent theologians and historians were brought in to examine the picture and to sift through any past evidence of ill-doing. Things were discovered. Two years after the paintings were completed, a janitor was contracted to clean Munkácsy's studio. After spending three hours with the paintings, he returned to his home and killed his wife and slit his own throat. A few weeks after that, a priest was given a tour of Munkácsy's studio. He returned to his church and burned a pile of Bibles and then leapt from the parapet to his death. Several other stories were unearthed. Eventually the paintings were returned from Prague to Hungary, and in 1955, the Deri Museum became their permanent home. Mr. Bocskai became the caretaker of the gallery and the teller of the painting's terrible history.

He told us the national arts council of Hungary had not seen any reason to limit the viewing of the paintings, and they had been on display in Debrecen for the past thirty years. But Mr. Bocskai said it had become his personal ordeal to describe to all visitors the painting's grim past and to prevail upon them to reconsider their desire to view the cursed object.

Our teachers unanimously decided we should return to Budapest immediately and leave the paintings undisturbed and unseen. We left the museum as quickly as we entered. I trailed a backward glance as we exited the dark confines of the dim halls and saw Mr. Bocskai nervously passing back and forth before the dark doors of the gallery, occasionally stopping to lay a head against the black, wooden door and mutter a silent prayer.

By the time we reached Budapest, many of us had forgotten the experience, as children will do. We returned to our gay lives and remembered very little of Mr. Bocskai's haunting tale. In fact, I recalled no further thoughts about the Munkácsy painting through the next many years of my life. Until, I regret to say, last week.

In my current job, I work for one of the many technology companies which dot the edges of Budapest's tech district. My job is to scour new websites and to assure their owners that there is no malware lurking anywhere in the twisted corners of the web programming. It was during one such episode of website work, a website devoted to tourism in Eastern Hungary, that I came across a chance fragment of a sentence regarding Munkácsy and his famed paintings.

Immediately, the childhood memory returned to me. I wondered, somewhat fancifully, what could have possibly frightened me so much. I decided, on a whim, to look up the painting in question, assuming, correctly as it turned out, that the paintings had long ago been scanned and uploaded and that images of it could be accessed online. Moments later I had the infamous image before me on my screen.

I spent a few moments poking around the large, scanned canvas, and soon I decided to rid myself of any doubt. I proceeded to zoom in, very far in, to the dark spot on the painting which Mr. Bocskai had spoken about so long ago. A moment later and Pilate's head hovered on my screen. And behind it, in dark pigments of brown and black, I saw the hollow.

For a moment nothing happened. I believed I had satisfied my curiosity and was just prepared to exit from the page. But then I sensed something. Or rather, I *heard* something. It was very low and incredibly quiet. Almost a whisper. But it was definitely a voice. And it said my name. For a moment I couldn't believe it. But then it repeated itself. I leaned in toward the screen. With my finger on my mouse, I zoomed in as far as the image would allow until my screen was saturated with nothing but dark pixels, quivering in the plasma of my monitor.

And then I saw them. Two eyes, open and terrible. They looked at me. They looked into me. And they said awful things to me. They told me to do things. To my friends. To my family. And finally, to myself. How long I stared into those eyes I cannot know. Finally, with a tortured howl, I pushed the monitor from my desk and saw, with great relief, the screen shatter as it struck the floor.

This was three days ago. And I have not been able to stop thinking about it. About those dark pixels and about the beast's eyes. What I have written here are my true recollections and my solemn testimony. When I have finished this document, I will post it on the bulletin boards and social passages of every network and webpage to which I have access. If you have come across this document, then it is hopefully for your own good that you are reading this.

What I write next I intend to come across with greatest gravity. Do not search for the painting. Do not seek it out. Do not find it. Do not look at the dark hollow. Do not permit what nests there to find you. Please do not.

Ramla Realizes

Co-Author Brent Larson

When my family still lived in Egypt I went to the only primary school in El Dahar, a city on the Red Sea coast. My friends and I grew up together, went to classes and birthday parties together, had the same crushes on the preparatory school boys. We teased and played. Life was great, even if I didn't know it yet.

One day our teachers taught us about the constellations, and which Egyptian deity matched with each and which ones marked our birthdays. I learned my birth god was Anubis, god of the dead. That's a nifty thing to say to a ten-year-old girl.

When I told my parents, my mom freaked out. "Little girls should not learn such things in school!" she said. My father, checking over test papers for his university students, looked at me over his horn-rimmed glasses, shrugged, and then went back to grading. The university in town where my father taught history had their own printing press. That night my dad showed me some pictures from one of the books printed at his university. The pictures were many different images of Anubis. There were also descriptions of the god next to each image. Apparently, he isn't just the god of the dead. He's also the god who embalmed the corpses before ushering them into the afterlife. One of the pictures showed Anubis holding a large scale in his hands. I asked my father what it meant. He translated the ancient characters which were carved into the stone next to the image. My father looked at me with raised eyebrows and said, "The scale was to weigh a person's heart, to see if they were worthy to accompany Anubis into the next world." We were both silent while I looked at the stony words in the picture. Then I brushed my teeth and went to bed.

One day our class went on a field trip to the Step Pyramid, a few hours south of where we lived. We took a bus which bobbed up and down on the dirt roads. When we reached the pyramid, a tour guide told us the stone structure of the pyramid was built by slaves and it took them over 100 years to complete. The pharaoh who designed the pyramid summoned builders from distant lands because during that time of Egyptian history most structures were made from mud bricks. The fact the pyramid was made from carved stone showed brilliant craftsmanship. The tour guide told us the pharaoh believed he had been blessed by the gods.

After the tour, the guide took us to a shop where snacks were sold. Near the shop there was a tunnel off to the side, leading below ground. One of the boys asked the tour guide where the tunnel went. The guide said the tunnel was off limits for guests because it was still being excavated; it led to the catacombs of Anubis. Everyone else went to the snack stand, but I wondered what I would see if I snuck down into the catacombs. I quickly slipped past the security tape when the guide wasn't looking, and soon I was running down a sandy slope, farther and farther below the sands of the desert.

There were a few lightbulbs strung along the tunnel on a piece of wire. I followed the lights, but with each step I grew more and more nervous. I kept expecting the tunnel would end, but it went on and on. Finally, I began to hear the sound of echoes ahead of me. I took a few more steps and then the tunnel gave way to a massive underground cavern. I looked up and what I saw took my breath away. It was the shape of Anubis with the black profile of a dog's head, high above me on the catacombs' ceiling. There must have been special windows cut into the ceiling, because slants of light came down and touched the ground around me. One bright shaft of light came directly from Anubis' eye. The light lit the ground where I stood. Wind from the desert whistled through the cavern. I felt like Anubis was looking at me. I was nervous because I had been away from my friends for so long. I turned and ran back up the corridor, all the way up to the snack stand. When I got there, one of my friends asked me where I had been. I told her I was using the bathroom. On the bus ride back to our school I took out my notebook and drew a picture of the figure of Anubis from the catacomb. I put my notebook down and as the bus bumped along I fell asleep.

I had a dream. In the dream I was in the catacomb. The sunlight came down from the ceiling, except this time it looked like the air around me was filled with glistening diamonds. The shape of Anubis on the ceiling slowly began to move. His head turned and this time I *knew* he was looking directly at me. He spoke. His voice was deep and seemed to come from the sands of the desert all around me.

He said, "I am your birth god. I chose you, Ramla."

That is one of the last memories I have of our time in Egypt. After that we moved to America, and everything got worse.

We moved to this dumb American suburb outside Edison, Utah, just after I turned 12. Dad got a job at the local American university because they wanted more foreign professors or something. So, I had to leave the El Dahar school system behind and start learning everything in American English. I remember my first day in middle school. Mr. Peterson, my English teacher said, "Class, welcome Ramla Adel! She comes here all the way from Egypt!"

He sounded so impressed. No one else was. My cheeks burned. I could hear the boys in the back of the room laughing. One of the boys pretended like he was calling out the call to prayer for Muslims.

Everything about life in American school was so different from Egypt. The food was different. The music was different. It didn't take me long to realize my body was different too. I guess I always had a thicker body, but all of the other girls in my Egyptian school did, too. I had never noticed before, but it didn't take long before I couldn't stop thinking about it. Even though cheerleading doesn't start for students in American school until high school, all of the ditzy blond girls in my class seemed to be in love with the cheerleader look. They all wore short skirts and close-fitting shirts, and they texted each other pics they found online of celebrities who they followed on their socials. The next few years went by pretty quickly. Even though I was surrounded by America, I never really felt like I fit in. I wished I could. I felt like I stuck out in the crowd like the foreign girl who didn't look right next to all these blond bodies.

In school we didn't learn about Egyptian gods anymore, but that didn't stop me from wishing I could get some help from Anubis. There's a boy named David in my class. I think he's gorgeous. I kind of wish I could get him to notice me, but he doesn't. I wish something would turn his eye toward me. I'm 17 now, and I could actually use some help from a divine being. I keep thinking about that time in the catacombs. I wonder if Anubis really looked at me that day. If he did, maybe he could help me? Maybe Anubis could turn David's eye? It couldn't hurt to wish for it. If I *could* wish for something, maybe I should start by asking for help with my body.

My face is so round. I hate it. No matter how I turn in the mirror I can't see any sculpted lines. That's what they call it on this beauty website all the girls go to – 'sculpted lines.' There are so many beauty definitions on that site that I don't have. "Cut stomachs," "firm thighs," "buns of steel." Um, no, no, and no. I don't have any of that. Nothing sculpted at all. There is no definition to my chin. I have no cheekbones.

I go to Edison High School, which is a lot like middle school because everyone still just cares about football and basketball and malls and tight bodies. In middle school the kids used to make fun of me because of my accent, my clothes, and my figure. By now I've figured out which clothes to wear, and I've lost the accent, but I still have the figure.

Once I told my parents how the kids treated me. "We all have to make sacrifices," Dad said, sounding annoyed. Like I should remember how tough it was for him, now that he's making more money and his students call him "Doctor Adel."

Mom waited until he left the table. "Ramla, all the women in our family have bodies like yours. It's part of your heritage." She was talking about my extended family back in Egypt. I wondered, not for the first time, if my mom knew her own face was full. She probably had never thought about it. She was classically beautiful, but no one from any extended family would say the same thing about me. Mom told me Egyptian women were supposed to carry themselves like queens. She said the Egyptian female body is designed to give birth to dynasties.

She obviously had never been to my gym class. Desert dynasties don't matter there. *David* doesn't care about dynasties. I told her the only girls I see around me are these cookie-cutter, blond, texting, fake, air-kissing Barbies. "Try making friends with these girls," Mom said. "You get them on your side, it'll make you feel like you belong here, Ramla."

Mom didn't get it. Those girls didn't care about me. They didn't want to be my friends. They all wanted the same thing, to stand out in a crowd. To be noticed. Well, what can I say, I wanted that, too. I wished for it. Sometimes at night I prayed for it.

My name "Ramla" means "one who realizes the future." That's was a joke. Even my name seemed like it was mocking me. If I could really realize the future, I would definitely make some changes. But it was increasingly clear that wasn't going to happen. I didn't foresee being happier. I couldn't foresee anything.

And then there was Sandra. She moved here from California last month. When our English teacher introduced her to the class, all the boys sat up straighter. David definitely noticed her right away. The afternoon sunlight lit up her cheekbones perfectly. *Someone* had sculpted lines. How was David NOT to notice her? The other thing about Sandra was she didn't wear a bra. Once Mr. Peterson asked the class for a declarative sentence for the English lesson. Sandra said, "Bras are a tight strap of patriarchy which depress women's sexuality and lower their place in society." Nice, Sandra.

Mr. Peterson asked for another declarative sentence example from the class, and a thought flashed through my mind. *Anubis chose me*. I'm so glad I didn't say it out loud. Nobody in high school wasted any time thinking about their birth gods. They were too busy liking each other online and seeing how many people commented on their posts. It was hard to see your future in the night sky when your eyes were focused on your phone.

I can't blame David for drooling over Sandra. They're made for each other. He's kind of perfect himself. He's got a face that's smiling and not mean, and completely free of acne. He's tall and he's on the football team, but he doesn't make fun of me like his friends. I've had a crush on him since middle school. So do half the girls in school. Not long ago, Sandra sent him some of her top-shelf selfies… just because she could. That certainly got his attention. If I tried to take a selfie of my upper body I wouldn't be able to get all of it in the frame.

It wasn't just the boys with Sandra, either. The girls were sucking up to her before her first week was out. I heard her talking to a bunch of them in another one of my classes a few days later, after one of them pointed out all the silver bracelets she wore. She said everyone in L.A. wore them that way. She sounded bored. And of course, a few days later, half the girls were wearing them too.

I found myself hating her a lot whenever I saw her. But I remembered what Mom said about making friends. I thought I should try. So, when English class was finished I followed Sandra up the hallway, watching her ponytail slide back and forth across her back, like a metronome. I was kind of hypnotized.

She got to her locker, and another girl, Theresa, was waiting for her. I've known Theresa for a few years. We've been friendly if not exactly friends. They started jabbering until Theresa saw me and stopped. Sandra turned around and got this little smirk. "Yes?" she said.

"I, uh," I suddenly realized I didn't know what to say. "I just wanted to say hi. I'm Ramla." I held out my hand like a moron.

"Well, hi-i-i-i!" She said, with this sing-song, high-pitched laugh that was totally put on. "Oh, your English is so good!" I didn't know what to say, and, instead, I kept standing there with my hand out, frozen. Sandra ignored my hand and turned back to her locker, and she and Theresa both laughed. I felt like such an idiot. I dropped my hand and took a couple steps back. I couldn't believe it.

And then David walked right by me. He seemed hypnotized, too. He walked up to Sandra and they started talking. I couldn't really hear what they said, but I think he asked her to the Freshman Formal. He also stared at her chest a lot.

Right before I turned and left, I saw Theresa staring at me. She had the same identical smirk as Sandra. And somehow, I knew I'd see it on the faces of all the girls at school before the week was out. Mom was wrong. There were no friends for me here. I felt so angry.

On the bus ride home, I pulled out my phone. I checked my socials. Someone posted a picture of me they took when I was trying to shake Sandra's hand. They used some kind of graffiti app to add some crude drawings of pyramids behind me and made it look like I was riding on a camel. The picture had dozens of likes. There were several comments underneath, all from anonymous commentators. The worst comment said, "Miss California meets the Cow of Sheba." Any wonder why I hate it here?

At home I stared at the walls for a couple hours, then finally decided to start my history homework. We were supposed to write a paper that described our personal family history. I started to google some information about El Dahar, and that's when I saw the web advertisement. Google must have figured I could read and speak Arabic because one of the first search results was for an Egyptian weight loss pill. It was called Tawahal, which means "transform." The slangy Arabic in the ad made the pill sound like it was different from other weight loss products. *"Magical measures…bury your old self!"* Something about removing water from the body and ancient Egyptian healing. I was curious so I clicked on it. They delivered to the United States, but shipping was over $100. Forget that!

It didn't take me long to get bored with my history homework. I looked out the window. It was getting dark. I went into the backyard and laid down on the grass so I could see the night sky. That was the one thing I liked about living in Edison. I could see the stars. Most nights I could even see the clear image of the Anubis constellation in the dark sky. Back in El Dahar there was too much pollution. But here I felt like I could sort of lose myself in the darkness above. Tonight, Anubis was particularly brilliant. The stars twinkled, like they were diamonds set in a perfect ring of dark resin. It reminded me of something else that weight-loss ad said: *"Embalm Yourself in Beauty."* That made me think of something else my primary school teacher taught me about Anubis, my constellation god. His name has more than one meaning. He was also *"He who fixes the future in the stars."* It seemed like more than a coincidence. If only Ramla meant more than just "One who realizes the future." Why couldn't my name mean, "One who makes the best future happen!?" Then maybe I could order that Tawahal pill and finally change into something completely different.

I finished looking at the stars and went to bed.

I woke up in the morning and checked my phone even though I knew I shouldn't. There were many more nasty comments on the picture of me and Sandra. Some anonymous commentator recopied the pic down below in the comments and when the picture popped up there was a vocal recording of some Middle eastern cleric giving the call for prayer.

I kept scrolling. Then I stopped and stared. I couldn't believe it. The next comment was from Sandra herself. She wasn't even trying to hide her name. She wrote, "Assalaam-Alaikum with extra 'ass' anyone?"

I threw my phone across the room and grabbed my laptop. A second later I was staring at the weight loss advertisement. I hovered the cursor over the buy button. I looked up at the ceiling, wishing for some kind of direction. What should I do? Then, my mouth slowly fell open. Just after we moved to America mom helped me decorate my room. We stuck glow-in-the-dark stars on my ceiling so I could see them at night. Now, even though it was morning, a ray of sunlight bounced off my bedroom mirror and reflected on the plastic stars. From the angle I was sitting the stars made a shape that looked just like the profile of Anubis. The head of a dog in profile with one plastic star shaped like his dark eye looking off to the side. Looking…right at me?

In that moment I suddenly felt like I was back in the catacombs beneath the desert. It felt so real, I almost imagined I could smell the dry scent of sand. It felt like a sign. I bit down on my lip, looked back down at my laptop, and clicked the button. I ordered the Tawahal. I used the pre-filled information for Mom's credit card. She wouldn't check it before the order went through, and then I would have to make something up. But by then I'd have it. It looked like the $100 shipping would really work. It was coming all the way from Egypt, but it said it would arrive tomorrow!

As far as I was concerned it couldn't get here fast enough. All day long in school people either snickered at me behind my back or looked at me with sympathetic useless glances. Everybody had seen the comments online. Mr. Peterson decided to use the occasion as an opportunity to try to shame the anonymous commenters. He said, "When one of us suffers, everyone suffers." I kept my eyes on the floor. He didn't say my name, but he may as well have. I felt like everyone's gaze was on me. In that moment I wished I was under the desert again, far from everyone's eyes.

Then, in gym class Sandra asked Mrs. Hutchins, our gym teacher, for shorts that were two sizes too small. In the locker room I snuck a peak of her squeezing into them. What can I say? They worked. When she came out of the locker room I could almost hear everyone's jaw hit the floor. She bent over to do some stretches. The waistband in her shorts eased itself lower with each stretch until her thong underwear was peeking over the top of the fabric. Then she stood up and pretended she had just noticed. "Ooops!" she said and covered her mouth with her hand, giggling.

She strutted over to David and stretched in front of him for a couple of minutes. Then I heard her ask for help with her English homework. He said yes. She said thanks and batted her eyelashes at him. But his eyes weren't on her lashes, they were on her hips.

I asked for permission to leave class to go to the bathroom. I spent the rest of that period locked in one of the stalls trying to fight back tears. When the bell rang I went to the sink to clean myself up. I looked at myself in the mirror. My fat face stared back at me, streaked with tears. I thought, "I am Ramla. And I have no future to realize."

The next day the Tawahal pills arrived. That really was fast! They came in a kind of elegant, expensive velvet box. The outside of the box was dark red with pictures of stars and moons and the inside was bright yellow with lots of images of the sun. A clever take on the name…a transformation from night to day. The inside of the box smelled faintly like dried hibiscus, like my mother's tea. For some reason it made me think of night breezes, blowing over the open desert. It reminded me of the catacombs.

Inside the box was a bottle of deep purple glass. The only other thing in the package was a list of ingredients…intybus, angustifolia, apricot kernel, zeolite. I didn't know what any of that stuff was. The instructions said to only take one pill per day. Then, in fancy lettering, there was another set of instructions. The lettering looked elegant and old. It was written in Arabic and English. It said, *"Hark, manifest through thought that which is desired."* I didn't really know what that meant. It sounded like I was supposed to meditate or something. Was I supposed to imagine what I wanted? I got a glass of water and took out a pill. It was small and white. I placed it on my tongue and swallowed it.

I went out into the backyard. I could see the Anubis constellation. It might have been my imagination, but it seemed even brighter than usual. I lay down on the grass. I imagined the Tawahal pill in my body. I pictured it dissolving and spreading throughout my skin. I tried to imagine the kind of body I wanted. I wanted my legs and hips to shrink. I wanted my stomach to dissolve like the pill. I wanted perfectly proportioned breasts. I wanted to look special. I wanted exotic beauty. I wanted to look like a princess from another land. I looked at the stars and pictured myself, my body. I also thought about Sandra; I couldn't help it. I kept remember the image of me trying to shake her hand in school. My faced flushed when I thought about all the horrible comments underneath. I felt anger rising in me when I pictured Sandra's face. I thought about her in those ridiculous tiny shorts. How would she like it if people laughed at her? How would she feel if those shorts shrunk and crushed her body? Then I surprised myself. I laughed out loud.

Finally, I looked at the Anubis cluster again. I saw the dark, sideways eye of the god. I imagined him looking down at me.

"Please," I prayed. "Please?"

When I woke up in the morning I lay there wondering what was wrong. I usually avoid touching my tummy because I hate that jiggling, but as I moved my hands across my belly it felt, well…firmer. I went to the bathroom and looked at myself in the mirror. I could tell immediately - my face looked different. I've spent years of my life staring at my face, trying to wish that flat fullness away. When I was nine, my dad once introduced me to one of his work friends as "my little full moon-face." They both laughed. I've always had a full face. And now? No, it wasn't my imagination. Today it was thinner! And it was smooth, with the slight hint of cheekbones. Wow! Sculpted lines! And there was something else.

I leaned in closer. My eyes shifted back and forth as I looked at my face. Then I held my eyes still and looked into them. A little breath caught in my mouth. It almost seemed like it was someone else was looking at me through my eyes.

Then, the light in the bathroom flickered, just a bit. The shadows of the objects on the sink lengthened, like they were lit from a light coming from the mirror. But that was impossible, wasn't it? The only thing in the mirror was…my face.

Yes! The light *was* coming from my face. It was as though my face had an otherworldly glow. I slowly turned my face from side to side and the shadows on the sink shifted back and forth, like they were dancing with me. As I stared at the mirror, the rest of the bathroom sort of faded into the background. Almost as though the lights were turned down on everything else except me. My skin was shining and there was a sharpness in my eyes that was a little scary…but also exciting. I've always felt like I was on display, but for the first time in my life, I wasn't ashamed. Usually I wanted to hide my Egyptian skin when people looked at me. But now I felt strangely different. I actually wanted people to see me. David, in particular.

I felt courageous. I needed to do something to stand out in school today. I decided to wear a dress today instead of jeans. I only had two. I picked the yellow one. Yellow like the sun, I thought. To match my transformation? Oh, I hoped so!

Usually at school I would go to the bathroom and wait until class was just about to begin, and then I would run in at the last minute so I could avoid everyone. Not today. Today I got to class early. In English class I sat in the front row, next to where Sandra usually sits. Mr. Peterson came in with his arms filled with English books. When he saw me he smiled and said, "Very bright today, Ramla!" Then he paused and looked at me more closely. "Did you get a new haircut or something?"

I shook my head with a little smile. He turned to his desk and sat down, making a few notes in his grade book. He kept taking little glances at me and shaking his head like he was trying to figure out what was different.

Then the rest of the class began to arrive and, even though I kept my eyes forward, I could sense everyone noticing me. I could hear whispers and feel glances. Finally, Sandra and David came in. The moment David looked at me he stopped talking and just stared. Sandra stared too. David sat behind us and halfway through class I felt something brush the back of my arm. I looked down. David was handing me a note!

I opened it. It said, "Damn girl nice dress!!"

I looked back at him and…it was very weird, but I kind of felt a jolt of electricity. Like I had a little bit of power coursing through me. And once again, like in the bathroom, I felt a flicker in the light around me. It seemed like time slowed down for a second. The shadows in the room lengthened. I saw the soft glow coming from my face touch David's face as he looked at me. His eyes widened. I lowered my head and stared into his eyes. His mouth slowly dropped open.

"David!" Sandra whispered. She sounded mad. I didn't look at her. Neither did David.

That night, I went out to the backyard again. There was no doubt. The Anubis constellation was intensely bright, far brighter than usual. The starlight was actually casting shadows through the branches of the trees. The shadows bent back and forth as a gentle breeze blew through the leaves. As I looked up at the sky, the world in my peripheral vision began to ripple gently, like eddies in a stream. I lay on the grass and felt the sensation of the earth revolving below me as the dark expanse of space passed by above.

Once again, I remembered myself, as a ten-year-old girl, standing in the catacombs of the Step Pyramid. I closed my eyes for a moment and imagined the feeling of cool walls of sand all around me. They gently exhaled an earthy smell that enveloped me, a scent of another land across the oceans. I remembered looking up at the sunlight shafting through the cut windows in the catacombs ceiling. I saw the dark profile of Anubis with his crafty sideways eye. The eye looked deep into my mine, deep into my soul. I felt him. I smiled with my eyes closed. I felt shadows of the moon slowly playing across my new smooth face.

I don't know how long I lay there. Finally, I got up. I went back my bedroom. I placed another Tawahal pill on my tongue and swallowed it. I imagined it dissolving within me. I lay on my bed and looked at the plastic stars on my ceiling. They, too, seemed brighter tonight, lit from below…lit from my face.

I fell asleep.

That night I had another strange dream. I was at the pyramid again. I had just come out from the catacombs. The night sky was brilliant with purples and blues and dark shadows of black, undulating and swirling in the cosmos. The stars flashed and circled like a time-lapse video. Only I was still as the world revolved around me. I walked forward into the desert.

Then I saw her. Sandra. She was huddled before me in the sand. But she was small…almost like she was a little doll. The doll was dressed in a tiny version of her gym outfit. I reached down. She tried to run away, but she wasn't fast enough. I picked her up and held her body in the air, silhouetted against the stars and moon. Her tiny arms and legs moved against my fingers as she tried to wiggle free.

Then, in my dream, I felt a choice emerge before me. As I looked at this tiny figure of Sandra I realized I could pity her…or I could hate her. I held the choice in my mind, like it was a scale of justice. Pity or hate? Then, I began to squeeze. Her body writhed and twisted, desperate to escape from the pressure of my hand. I felt her bones break and snap like twigs. Her writhing slowly stopped. Her skin dried in my hand. I could smell a potpourri of desiccated flowers floating up to my nostrils. Roses, lilacs, hibiscus. I felt tiny granules of sand and dried leaves against my skin. A moment later the Sandra-dust in my hand floated up into the dark sky in a tiny cloud. There was a deep moan from the stars above as her dust drifted up into the sky toward the Anubis cluster. The dust disappeared into his dark eye, flickering as it disappeared, the eye winking at me.

In the morning when I looked at myself in the mirror, I couldn't believe it. I was looking at two different people. It was me…and it was someone else. My face was entirely mine but richly different. As I stared into the mirror I felt the imperceptible flicker in the lighting around me again. The shadows lengthened as I looked deeply into my eyes. In my hazel irises I saw the same fearful, little-girl eyes that had been with me back in Egypt, in El Dahar, in my elementary school, through all those past years. Those were the same little eyes that looked up at the ceiling of the catacombs so long ago. But those eyes in the mirror that day were also someone else's. And this new woman…I didn't know who she was. Her eyes were darker. The eyes were still hazel, but there seemed to be smoldering fires burning in the brown depths. These new eyes seemed alive, but where there should have been dewy liquid glistening instead there was something remote and dry, the unblinking sockets of a statue. They seemed ancient and regal. These eyes belonged to another woman. If she was a woman? She seemed…somehow more than flesh and blood. Yet there was no denying her beauty. My beauty, I thought, with a smile. I kept turning and looking at my body, and with each turn it was like I was seeing a voluptuous hourglass of olive skin revolving and shifting before my eyes.

"Ramla, have you done something with your hair?" Mom asked at breakfast. She made waffles – Dad insisted we eat traditional American food as soon as we moved here – but I didn't eat much. I wasn't hungry. Usually I had a good appetite. This was odd. But, perhaps it wasn't so strange. Perhaps I wasn't hungry? Something in me was changing. I could feel it.

I skipped class and spent the day on my computer, googling words: Anubis… Tawahal… Ramla… Egyptian mythology… magic ingredients… anything I could think of. I learned about a lot of things. The ingredients for Tawahal, for example. Most of them were natural herbs. But apricot kernel is sometimes used to make cyanide. And zeolite is used in desiccant packets to keep clothes from getting musty. Its main purpose is to dry and preserve something to its intended state.

I also searched the instructions that came with the pills. They were taken from an ancient Egyptian text called *The Wisdom of Anubis*. The text is supposed to provide fortune to those who quote from it and spite to one's enemy. It was part of the Osiris myth, where Anubis allows the queen, the wife of Osiris, to restore her husband's body through mummification. The myth revolves around the concepts of order and disorder, sexuality and rebirth, death and afterlife. Quoting from it is supposed to grant the speaker's deepest desires.

According to Anubis mythology, Osiris's wife not only managed to perfectly embalm her husband's body, but, in doing so, she permanently changed herself as well. The chemicals she used in the mummification process deeply poisoned the skin on her hands. She went down to the waters of the Nile the next day to soak her hands and seek some relief. But when she placed her hands in the water, the river gave off a hiss like droplets of water when they strike a hot iron. The waters shrank from her touch. The queen returned to the palace, shutting herself in her chambers and ordering no one to disturb her. For the next week there was no sound from behind her doors. When her servants finally and fearfully entered her chambers, they found her body frozen, perfectly preserved as though beneath a sheen of amber, with her eyes still wide open and a life-like smile permanently frozen on her pink lips. That year, the Nile delta region endured the greatest drought of the past hundred years.

The ancient Egyptian text which I translated said that next fall, after the Nile delta drought, there was a new star which appeared in the Anubis cluster, right in the center of the god's dark eye. The royal astrologers believed the new star was the queen herself, now permanently with her god in the night sky.

I wrote some lines in my notebook. As the words played over in my mind and onto the page, I felt a familiarity there, like someone who remembers a language they once forgot. And again, I felt like I was someone else. Like Ramla Adel was someone familiar who I just met for the first time.

When I searched some more, I found some ancient Egyptian poetry attributed to the queen. She supposedly wrote it during those final days in her chamber. One of the lines said, *"I held the choice in my hand."*

The next day in school I walked by David and Sandra in the hallway. Sandra was wearing something slutty and obnoxious. David caught my eye and he froze in mid-sentence. Sandra glared at me. I felt almost embarrassed for her. Almost. I pictured the scales in my hands again. Pity…or hate?

That evening I went out under the stars again. If I didn't see it for myself I wouldn't have believed it. The shadows practically raced across the back yard as the sky seemed to swirl above me in its time lapse dance. I didn't need to look up to know the Anubis cluster was blazing. The backyard seemed as bright as daytime. I held out my hands and watched the shadows play across my new skin. I pictured the queen dipping her hands into the river waters and seeing them shrink before her.

I took out my notebook and by the light of the stars I began to read softly,

"Whoever knows this spell…she will be like Osiris in the netherworld.

She will go down to the circle of fire. She will open the portal! She will touch the flame!"

Who am I? Who will I be tomorrow? I asked myself as I took a Tawahal pill and lay down in my bed. My body was vibrating as I fell asleep. I was not afraid.

I woke up earlier than usual and went directly to the mirror. I took off all my clothes and just stood there. My skin was flickering and pulsing like dappled sunlight. Something was moving almost imperceptibly beneath my skin…lightly shifting like blown sand. My mouth was a full set of ruby lips. I looked deep into my eyes. Into her eyes. I lost myself in her dark reflection and saw a brilliant desert splayed out before me, perfectly preserved behind glass.

I wore my other dress. The red one with the beaded belt.

I didn't go into English class. Instead, when the buzzer rang, I stood in the center of the hallway. When the students came out of their classes they turned to look at me as they passed…my body was parting them like the flowing waters of a river around a jeweled island. David came up the hall toward me. When he saw me, he dropped his books. I walked toward him, and my island moved with me, everyone at arm's length. David started to say something, but I held up my finger. He stood there, wide-eyed. I gave a little smile and touched my finger against his lips. The saliva on his lips was wet beneath my finger, and then it dried under my touch.

And then I heard behind me her voice, "You! You get away from him!"

Everyone froze in mid-stream. I turned slowly. Sandra was wearing a tiny t-shirt and a miniskirt that barely seemed to contain her. She also had these long, strappy high heels. She looked like a badly dressed Barbie doll with clothes that have been stretched on and off too many times to count. She came toward me. My island widened to accommodate her.

I took a step towards her. She was visibly shaking.

"Hi, Sandra," I said. My voice was dusky and low. Sassy with a hint of malice in its depths.

Her eyes widened and she threw down her books. She cocked her arm back and swung at me full force. I drew back just a few inches and the strike missed. Then she was off balance, wobbling on her heels, and she fell against me. Her t-shirt caught on my beaded belt and tore away with a prolonged rip.

Everyone gaped as she screamed and threw her arms across her bare chest. Cell phones came out. People were snickering. I could practically feel the socials fill up with echo upon echo of her repeated picture branding itself across the net, copying itself into eternity. I wondered how she felt about bras and the patriarchy in that moment. Strangely, the thought left my mind as soon as it came. I seemed above it now. It felt like I was looking down on this high school scene with the disinterested gaze of a queen who sat high above her subjects. It seemed like those lowly juvenile thoughts were wisping their way across a gulf of thousands of years. Rising to affix themselves to the constellation of Anubis.

Sandra stared up at David, who was still behind me, standing still like a statue. Her mascara was running down her face, making her look like a raccoon. Her eyes flicked back to me. Her breath hitched a few times, then finally caught. "WHO DO YOU THINK YOU ARE?!" she screamed.

"I know who I am," I said. I turned, and the sea of students again parted before me. I felt power come off my body. And, for the first time, I realized it was true. I knew exactly who I was.

I took two Tawahal pills that night. The floor beneath my feet in the bathroom was shifting sand on a beach. I walked to the mirror. The girl looking back at me looked like a dark princess with wind swirling around her like a mirage. I could hear deep voices chanting and churning. I looked into her eyes, my eyes. I saw the desert within them. My desert. My home.

That night I dreamt I was floating above a desert floor. The sand below me was covered with thousands of people who had come to gaze up at me. They brought offerings … baskets of dried flowers and crushed leaves. Intybus and belladonna and myrrh. Jerusalem leaves and pyrena shells and thorny resin. They laid them at my throne as they bent down in reverence. On the horizon was a storm with flashes of lightning, coming closer. In the thundercloud it seemed like a constellation of stars was moving and growing. It looked like Anubis.

When I awoke in the morning I did not look in the mirror. There was no need.

My clothes in my closet were all gone. They were replaced with regal garments and beaded strands of pearls. A gift from Anubis. I chose the transparent purple sari. I slipped it on and felt the dry fabric slide effortlessly across my marbled skin. I looked in the mirror. I blinked and my hair was immaculately fixed into a towering mountain of black curls with winks of pearls and jewels laced throughout.

When I walked out the front door of my house the people in my neighborhood were all lined up on each side of the street, waiting for me. They were all naked. As I walked down the street, the people bent and swayed and moaned softly. The sun shown in the sky, but only briefly, as twilight fast came after it, the movement of the earth meaningless now in this new world flowing out and unfurling around me.

I walked down the street. Row after row of people gathered, bowing. I passed the high school. My teachers were all bent at the waist, naked like everyone else. Mr. Peterson held a copy of our literature textbook in his hand, its dry pages fluttered in the desert breeze. I went to the highest hill in the downtown city park. The rest of the town had already gathered there, their heads tilted back in a rictus of admiration as they stared up at me. Mother and Father were there, also naked. Father's eyes were downcast, and he looked as one utterly debased. Mother smiled timidly. *Oh Mother*, I thought. *We are no longer in El Dahar or Edison or any other place which came before. This is my new world. The desert is my palace. I give the commands and I choose the paths. I have no use for friends. Only for those who worship.*

As I waited I saw a column of people carrying a funeral pyre. Sandra's desiccated body was on it. Her eyes looked crusted and white. The cyanide had leaked from her eyes and dried there like salt. Her legs and arms stuck out at odd angles as though the bones within were broken and set poorly. As her pyre was brought nearer people around her crowded in, their eyes on me, waiting for the command. Several people were already carrying lit torches.

As I looked down on everyone, I opened my mouth and a low call rolled out from my chest. Soon the town was writhing and holding their hands up towards me. The torches touched the pyre and Sandra's body succumbed to flame. I saw David in the midst of the crowd. I beckoned. The crowd prodded him forward up the hill. When he reached me, I turned to the attendants on either side of me. They removed David's clothes and wound a linen cloth around his hips. The attendants brought him to me. I took him into my arms and felt a great power surge within me, as though a billion voices were stored within my heart. I pointed to the night sky which swirled above us. I pointed at Anubis.

There was a crack like lightning. With a huge smile Anubis turned his massive dark head in the sky and looked me full in the eyes. A bright white flash tore from the heavens and the town below me dissolved into sand. Nothing was left but a magnificent desert. The heat was brilliant, intense, and Anubis's eye rays penetrated my skin, suffusing it. I breathed in deeply. There was a wetness on my cheeks, and I realized the torrid air had liquified my eyes. And yet I could see more clearly than ever. Everything was tinged with gold. My human eyes dripped down my face. In their place, deep in sockets of gold, my new eyes formed. In their dark, hazel depths were eons of ancient history, now, alive again, radiant and waiting to be born afresh.

In a split second the sun, moon, and stars tore across the sky a million times in a flash and fled beyond the horizon. The old sky was replaced with a new sky. A night sky absolutely inflamed with stars, the brightest of which was the Anubis cluster with its dark, central, beckoning eye. I continued to breathe and I felt the light of day and night enter my eyes, my face, my waiting body.

I suddenly knew things, dark things, ancient things. I understood. I stood before the world, a cosmic Pharaonic queen. I contained within me all love…Sapphic, Achillean, Eros. I watched as all previously people were born, lived, met, loved, coupled, dissolved, and died. All the world bowed before me. Anubis, God of the Dead, Embalmer, rested his scepter on my brow.

"Why me?" I asked, through lips frozen, carved into a smiling sarcophagus of eternal devotion.

"I called you," Anubis answered. "You heard my voice. You searched for me in my catacombs beneath the sand. You found me."

I am Ramla. I have become my name. I have realized my future.

Alice and Roses

Alice had no internet at home, so every morning at 10 she walked to the public library to check her email. But the Stephanie hadn't written yet. It had been two weeks.

Yesterday when she was ordering her coffee, Alice talked a bit with the young lady behind the counter, and Alice told her about Stephanie. "She's got so much on her mind," Alice had said. "It isn't an easy decision, you know. Moving across the city. And she's never lived anywhere but uptown before. You know how people are. She's so used to uptown. She's quite busy. That's probably why I haven't heard from her yet."

As Alice walked toward the library she thought, with a small smile, about Stephanie. Alice wondered if Stephanie was thinking about her.

She began to reassure herself of all of the reasons why Stephanie had not written yet. She was definitely busy with her job. She probably didn't have a spare moment to herself when she was working. She certainly must be carefully considering the proposal. Such things mustn't be rushed. Haste makes waste and all. She would be over the moon with endless thoughts. She might, at any moment of the day, need to pause her typing and dab at her face with a Kleenex so that her beads of perspiration wouldn't alert her boss to any worries or doubtful strayings of her mind.

It was just over two weeks ago that Alice had written to Stephanie asking her whether they might move in together. It took her over an hour to compose the email. She labored over it fairly diligently. She thought Stephanie would be thrilled with the offer, but she suspected Stephanie might have certain natural worries about how exactly everything should proceed. She was already comfortably living in her apartment across town. And there was the matter of their long-absent acquaintance with each other. That would require a certain degree of nurture and warming as all long-dormant relationships do.

She had typed the email very carefully. She said she was happy they hadn't tried to move into any serious relationship territory in college because they both had so much to learn. She wrote how thrilled she was they had met again now, after they each had time to experience the world on their own terms and finally realized what they needed all along in life.

She said that she was happy for them to live in her apartment, or, should Stephanie prefer it, Alice could move in with her. Stephanie lived in one of the new uptown lofts which was near to the print shop where Alice ran into her last month.

Last month Alice had gone into the print shop because she wanted to make copies of a newspaper article she read that morning. The print shop in her neighborhood was being painted, and so she took a bus across town to the print shop which, as it turned out, was just around the corner from Stephanie.

She had tried to explain to Stephanie why she was there that day, making copies of articles from the newspaper. Every few days she would find an article she disagreed with and she pasted up copies of the newspaper piece around her apartment building and on the street corners of her block. She felt it was a kind of civic duty she owed to the people of her neighborhood. If she didn't bring their awareness to the problems of the world then perhaps they would never be discovered and then where would the world be? She had just been running off the final copies when she had spied Stephanie across the room. Stephanie was in the print shop making copies for her boss.

Alice had walked up to her and tapped her a friendly hello on the shoulder. Stephanie turned in a skittish manner and had a vacant stare on her face as she looked at her. She had acted like she didn't really remember her. Alice told her about college and she reminded her of the classes they had together. She scratched her head and then smiled a faint smile and told her sure she remembered Alice now.

Stephanie had hurried out of the print shop without looking back. Alice had finished her copies and, on her way out the door, she glanced down at the floor and saw Stephanie had dropped her business card in her haste. She had picked it up and slowly traced her finger along the words of her name. She also passed her eyes along the contact information. That is where she had gotten her email address.

Alice was lost in these thoughts when she heard the lock click on the library's front door. The custodian who opened the doors smiled at Alice in a somewhat bored manner. The custodian went back into the building, and Alice followed him.

Alice found her regular computer in the front row, the third one down. She flicked on the power button and waited while the machine hummed itself awake. Alice quickly typed in her password. She made a mistake and needed to type a second time. Finally, the inbox hovered to life in front of her.

Her smile dimmed, but just a bit. Stephanie hadn't written again today. Alice gave a little shrug. This was rather like her, she thought. She smiled. It might even be a kind of little game.

Alice glanced over at the computer next to her. Odd. The computer screen was on. Usually they were off in the morning before the doors opened. A screensaver image of a flower slowly floated across the screen. Alice looked around. No one else was using the computers. Why was this one on? Oh, well, she thought, someone must have forgotten to turn it off the night before. She stood up to leave, and, as she was standing, her leg bumped the table and caused the mouse next to the neighboring computer to jostle. The screensaver disappeared and she saw a familiar email screen. It was the same email service as Alice's. Whoever had last used the computer yesterday must have been in the middle of an email session and forgotten to log out. She recognized the row of emails, starting with an email from today and then fading down into the past as the row got longer toward the bottom of the screen.

She also noticed there was an email from today which hadn't yet been opened. She didn't want to pry or anything, but it was impossible not also to notice that the email was addressed to someone named Peter and that it came from someone named Sylvia. She frowned a bit. Ah, well. Some people are absent-minded, of course. Things come up all the time. People forget things. People must rush home in the middle of the day and sometimes they forget their emails. This is what must have happened between Peter and Sylvia, whoever they were. And Peter must not be too careful, Alice thought. Peter must have changed his email settings to not require a password. Anybody could walk by and read the emails.

Not right, thought Alice. *Not proper behavior.* She reached forward and switched off her computer. She stood up and left the computer next to her as she had found it, with the email screen on and the Peter/Sylvia email yet unread and waiting.

When she got back up to her apartment the light on her telephone was flashing. She groaned silently. It would be from her mother. She walked over and pressed the message button on the phone. There was a moment of crackle and then her mother's voice began to speak.

"Hello, Alice," her voice said. "I'm not sure where you are. I was wondering if you might be free for dinner tonight? It's been a few weeks

since I saw you. I had a few questions about what Doctor Avery said…"
Click. Alice pushed the delete button. The red light disappeared. She
stared down at the phone for a few moments, feeling a tinge of anger
pulsing in a vein in her temple.

What did her mother know, she thought? What did anyone know,
after all? Certainly nothing helpful. And these calls! Always at all times of
the day. Always asking. Always pestering. Always coming up with some
reason why she was worried or why she was fretting over Alice again. It
was nonsense, she thought.

Stephanie would write tomorrow. She felt sure.

Tomorrow there was no response. Alice received a spam email
from a hardware company and a reminder from her mother that Alice had
not answered her email or her phone call from yesterday. She had asked
her something about the doctor again. But Stefanie had not written. She
frowned briefly as she ignored the spam and deleted her mother's email.

Alice looked back down at the email screen in front of her. She
glanced over at the computer next to her on the right, the one which hadn't
been turned off yesterday. It was still on. The screensaver flower drifted
across the screen slowly. It must have stayed on through the night. Alice
was curious. She looked around. No one was nearby. She reached off and
nudged the neighboring mouse and the screensaver disappeared. The same
email page appeared. And there was still the same unopened email for
Peter from someone named Sylvia waiting at the top of the stack.

Alice glanced up and down the row, wondering if Peter might be
here today. She didn't see anyone who looked like a Peter. Where could
Peter be? How could he leave his email open like this for anyone in the
world to see? How could he not have written back to Sylvia promptly and
with no nonsense or delay? There was no accounting for manners, Alice
thought. Certainly, emails come and go, but also just as certainly people
had a duty to answer them. When they involve important matters and have
something to do with future steps and important decisions, well, then they
need to be answered. It wasn't right of Peter to be like this, Alice thought.
Well, if Peter wasn't going to respond…

Alice glanced around her. The library was humming with the light
quiet buzz of many people going about their business. Nobody was

looking at Alice. She stood up quietly and slowly. After one more look around, she sat down in front of the computer on her right.

The highlighted email, the one which hadn't been opened yet, was glowing near the top of the screen. She could see from the preview text what was written at the beginning of the email. It said, "*Peter, my sweet love…*" Alice couldn't help but smile. She didn't know this Sylvia, but something about her seemed quite fetching.

Alice cautiously leaned forward. She let her hand waver for a moment in the air above the mouse. Then she allowed her hand to drop down and to curl around the plastic body of the mouse on its soft pad. For a moment, she hovered the cursor over the highlighted email on the screen. Then Alice pressed the button to open the email. There was a small animation and then the email was revealed.

Peter, my sweet love,

I have been ever so desperate to hear from you. It is really not right that you should make me wait so long. I only remind you because you yourself told me to write if you did not respond by Tuesday. Well, here it is, now Tuesday come and gone, and I certainly don't know what to do or what to think.

I spend all my days and every hour of them in a frightful twist. I've worn such a path in my rug with pacing, and all I can do is turn and fret with nowhere to go and nothing to do for fear that you might not have liked my proposal of Bermuda. I'm sure you know this, you fine specimen. Dearest, of course we don't HAVE to go, but Daddy's made the resort available for the whole week, and we'll never get another chance now that you've received your promotion.

Darling, if you could only just send me a short note then I would know that everything was fine. Until you do I shall be waiting with bated breath, and you must know that your dear anxious girl is desperate for your quick assurance waits for your every beautiful word.

Love, Sylvia

Alice read the email three times. The third time she read it very slowly, feeling each word in her mouth and head as she read it. After reading it Alice slowly let out a long breath and placed her hand on her chest. She closed her eyes. She could feel her heart beating quietly within her. The library hum faded into the distance and all she knew for a long spell was the soft assurance of the warm room holding her firmly on all sides.

As she closed her eyes she pictured this Sylvia. She pictured her as she must have looked, writing this email. How she must have agonized over it. And for so long! She saw her painted fingers flying across the keyboard in a terrible frenzy of emotion. She watched her flit her eyes across the words as she carefully chose what to write. She saw her chew on her nails, worried a particular phrase might scare Peter off. She watched her delete a phrase and replace it with one which more closely adhered to the feelings she kept for Peter in her heart.

Then she watched Sylvia send the email. Then Sylvia must have stood up in front her computer, in her apartment, wherever she lived. She would have walked over to the window and looked out at the sunshine. It must have been a beautiful day when she wrote that email. The sun was probably shining just so. It might have been during that special hour in the evening when everything was sharp and truly anything seemed possible.

Alice imagined Sylvia there, standing before her window, thinking about the email she had just sent. Alice saw her watching the sun. She saw the rays of sun coming through the clouds and she pictured the flight to Bermuda. And then, just for fun, Alice pictured herself as Peter. It wouldn't hurt, she thought. Peter obviously didn't care much for Sylvia or he would have answered the email. No. Peter was not for her.

So, in her thoughts, Alice saw herself next to Sylvia as they sat on the plane, waiting for the flight to Bermuda to take off. She saw herself holding Sylvia's hand as they sat, side by side, on the plane as it taxied from the terminal. The plane picked up speed as it roared down the runway. At the moment the plane took off into the air a slight bit of turbulence shuddered through the plane and Sylvia hid her face in Alice's shoulder. Alice lifted her hand and softly stroked Sylvia's hair. Her black hair.

Alice thought all these thoughts as she sat in front of Sylvia's open email with her eyes closed. She opened her eyes. She was smiling deeply. She slowly glanced around the library again. No one was watching. It was a very special moment, just then. She could tell. She could feel it intimately within herself.

She leaned forward. She typed,

My dearest Sylvia, please forgive me. The thought that I have left you so stranded with your thoughts devastates me. You are a precious creature, and you ought not to be made to wait so long. My riddling conscience pokes at me this very moment, prodding me to answer you.

The world is already so fraught with worry. Why needlessly spoil even one more day with confusion or twisted feelings? Hasn't enough been experienced? Aren't we masters of ourselves and of the path which winds before us? Sylvia, you and I have been wanderers. But now we have found each other.

But, yet, let me prolong the tension just a bit longer. It is so crude for us to attempt a connection like this through words on a screen. Can this really be the right way to settle something between us?

Let me risk offending you by asking whether you would allow me to deliver the news to you in person. Since we have already been apart for these many days perhaps a few more hours won't matter.

Would you consent to meet me tomorrow night? Will you believe in me? I believe in you.

But now, no doubt, you'll be wondering...where shall we meet? All the places we've been together before are colored by the experiences of our past. And our way forward will not be found in the past but in the yet-unrealized future. And you must see, as I do, that our path leads into new places, through new passes and mountain peaks not yet seen or explored.

Let me propose a new destination...I spied it out the other day on my morning walk. Naturally as I walked that morning my thoughts were filled with you. I pictured you as I walked, and I imagined where we might one day stroll together. I know it might seem to you a childish fancy, but I found a place for us to meet. Will you meet me tomorrow? I know the place.

The park on 6th Street, by the main entrance. There is a promenade which crosses through the park gardens, filled on all sides with fragrant blossoms and flowers from distant lands.

We could walk through those flowers. Near the center of the garden is a rose bush. It is nestled down among the many other fronds, and I know not many people have seen it themselves. I like to think of this rose bush as our special collection of flowers. I mean to take one of those roses from that bush and place it, plucked clean of thorns, behind your ear.

Then, on the far side of the park, there is a koi pond with a man who rents boats. Perhaps we could continue our time together by floating under the perfect, star-filled sky with the stars all reflected around us on the water and, yes, reflected as well in the deep pools of your eyes.

This is how I am picturing us together. Dare I tell you…I will…I am picturing it now as I write these words. And my heart is aching that it must wait even one more day to see you again. But, surely, the words of the poet ring so true as all informed truth does: 'Absence makes the heart…' Well, you know the rest.

So, let me wait for you tomorrow at the park entrance. Please be there. And, as a way to fulfill my childish fancy would you consent to wear a red scarf? Red, after all, is the color of deepest passion.

Will you meet me so? Will you come at eight? I know that I will be there.

Yours, Peter

She sat back and reread the email in one go. Then, with a smile, she clicked the button and sent the email to Sylvia.

She awoke with a deep glow of pleasure on her face. She slowly curled herself out of bed. She spent some time at her window, looking down at the street below. The many cars moving this way and that seemed to play a merry tune of sorts in their dancing movement to and fro.

She dressed, choosing her one red dress from the back of the closet. Her mother had insisted on buying it for her. She had never worn it before. She had never had need of it or occasion for it, until now.

As she was dressing the telephone rang. She thought about it, then decided. She walked over and picked it up.

"Alice?" her mother said.

"Hello, mother," she said.

"Oh, Alice, I'm so glad to hear your voice. I was worried. Didn't you get my other message?"

"Yes, mother."

She continued speaking. "Well, you gave me a fright, not answering me. And I wrote to you as well. Did you read that? It's about Doctor Avery. She had several thoughts and a good many suggestions, but I suppose the main thing is she wants you to switch what you're currently taking..."

Alice let her go on for a while. As she talked she drifted over to the window again and looked up at the sky. She looked at the clouds drifting by and pictured Sylvia's face in the pillow whiteness of their folds. She saw her waiting for her at the park with her red scarf. She saw her bending down among the flowers, finally laying down among them with her hands spread out on either side, letting the flowers envelop her. She lay there for a moment and then put her arms up to Alice, beckoning her to join her in the blossoms.

She walked back over to the telephone cradle and hung it up, cutting her mother off mid-sentence.

Alice left her apartment and walked down the stairs. She came out onto the street. She walked up the sidewalk in the direction of the library. As she walked she smiled at the people who passed by her. Everybody's face seemed delightful today, Alice thought. It really didn't take much, did it? People just needed confidence in themselves and in their hopes for the future. Silly, Alice thought. She could have told them that if they had asked her.

Alice walked up to the library. She nodded to the custodian and walked to the row of computers. She passed by the third one and sat down at the fourth. The screen was still on and the email box was still open from yesterday. Peter's email screen. And, yes, there was a new email waiting.

She glanced around the library again. She grabbed the mouse and opened the email. It said,

Peter, darling,

You are a mischievous one, aren't you? But, why cut about and make you wonder yes, of course I'll meet you. I'll be there promptly at eight. And I do believe I could scare up a red scarf just for you.

Whatever do you have in mind, you coy fellow?

Thank you, dearest!

Love,

Sylvia

Once again, she reread the email three times carefully. She smiled softly to herself. She stood. But, as she was preparing to leave, she glanced back down at the third computer, the one she usually used.

Why not, she thought? She sat down and switched it on. The screen warmed itself and soon the familiar box of her own email was hovering before her again.

She stared at the screen, not quite believing it. There was a new email. It was from Stephanie.

She grabbed the mouse and quickly clicked open the email. It said,

Hello, Alice,

I was very surprised by your email.

This is difficult to write, but I think you have misunderstood some things. I feel so sorry, but I cannot agree to your invitation.

I know this must be disappointing. You seemed very lonely when we spoke at the print shop. I feel you need someone to talk to, but I cannot be that person for you now.

Please take care of yourself.

Stephanie

Alice frowned as she read through the email the third time. There was so much Stephanie didn't understand. Alice could see this from her awkward tone and from her confusing manner. Alice could even imagine her typing it. Stephanie would have been hoping she didn't take things the wrong way. She must have been burdened by many things, work perhaps or with something she had heard from home. Parents were the worst. It was probably something Stephanie's mother said to her. Poor Stephanie, Alice thought. She hoped she would be well.

This made it all the better for her that things were going to work out with Sylvia. So many problems with the world, she thought. Too many people rushing about going on and on, only concerned with their own lives, never minding the fact that the world is filled with other people, not just themselves. Other people with needs and feelings.

Alice moved back over to the fourth computer and read through Sylvia's email again. She lingered thoughtfully over the final words, *"I'll be there promptly at eight. Thank you, dearest. Love, Sylvia."*

The day drifted by in hitches and puffs. After the library Alice went back to her block. She bought the paper and read through it in the coffee shop downstairs from her apartment. Today the articles in the paper did not disturb her as before.

She glanced up and saw the young girl behind the register. Perhaps she would like to know about her date with Sylvia. She stood up to walk over to her, but then disappeared into the back room. Ah, well, Alice thought. Not everybody understands these things. She went back upstairs to her apartment to wait.

The sun was dropping lower in the sky. She glanced at her watch. It was just after seven thirty. Where was Sylvia now, she wondered? Surely, she was on her way to the park. Surely, she would be there soon. She looked at herself in the mirror.

The phone rang. Alice ignored it and walked out the door.

She quickly walked down the stairs in her building and exited onto the street below. She stole across Fifth Street and walked quickly up Sixth until she reached the corner of the park. The park was near empty. There were just a few people walking in and out of the flower gardens within. Alice walked up to the main entrance of the park and looked around. There was no one here yet.

She moved across the street and sat down on the bench on the other side. From here she could see the entrance clearly. She looked again at her watch. It was quarter to eight.

From where she was sitting she could see people come and going through the main entrance of the park. Then, after a period, there was no one. Then a bus stopped on the corner. A young woman got out. She came walking up the sidewalk toward the park entrance. Alice followed her carefully with her eyes. As she came closer she could see quite clearly. She was wearing a red scarf.

Alice stood from the bench. She took a step toward the street and then stopped. She wanted to prolong the moment, just a bit. She watched Sylvia come closer until she reached the entrance. A few children on bikes raced by. Sylvia smiled at them as they rode by. Then she looked back and forth up the street. Alice carefully stepped behind a tree. She could see Sylvia, but Sylvia couldn't her yet.

She watched her. She was fascinated. Sylvia looked just like she imagined her. In fact, it was just as she had appeared in her dream. She was wearing a black skirt and a sharp blouse. Around her neck she wore a scarf which was dark red. She kept nervously adjusting her blouse and flicking her fingers through her hair which was loose and flowing, moving ever so slightly in the evening breeze.

Alice continued to watch. More minutes ticked by. Sylvia kept looking up and down the street. She could tell she was growing anxious. Once or twice she looked into the park. Finally, she looked up the street one last time and then turned and entered the park.

Alice moved out from behind the tree. She cautiously crossed the street. By the time she reached the park's entrance she could see Sylvia walking down through the park, past the rows of flowers in the flower garden. Alice quickly moved into the park and followed her.

Alice cut across several rows of flowers so she could see Sylvia moving from the side. She kept stealing glances back at the entrance. When she reached the center of the garden she began to hunt around among the various bushes. Then she stopped moving and stared. Although Alice couldn't see it from where she stood she knew Sylvia had found the rose bush. She stared at it for a long moment. As she did Alice began to move closer to her. Sylvia looked off in the direction of the pond. Her eyes seemed to be filled with an expression of longing and loss. She walked out of the flower garden toward the pond.

Alice could bear it no longer. Hadn't she let her wait long enough? Hadn't she better come to her and make everything right? She reached down and plucked a single rose.

She walked through the last rows of flowers. As she did she slowly picked off the thorns one by one, letting them drop to her side as she walked. Sylvia was standing with her back to her, looking out at the koi pond. Alice silently moved up behind her and stood just a foot from her back. She reached forward and softly passed her hand through the flowing black hair.

Sylvia immediately turned.

"Hello, Sylvia," Alice said as she held up the rose.

The Programmed Joy of Protection

Ruth sat carefully in the chair with her hands folded in her lap. Her straight, black hair was neatly pulled into a sensible ponytail. She looked directly at Mrs. Juvland as the older woman spoke. Ruth made sure to nod occasionally, and once she even gave a little "mm-hmm" to show that she was paying close attention.

"Well," Mrs. Juvland finally said, tapping the paper on the table, "I am very happy with this reference."

Ruth smiled and looked at the floor, a flush of embarrassed joy rising in her cheeks.

Mrs. Juvland continued, "I don't see any reason why you couldn't start this weekend."

Ruth looked up quickly. "Oh, please," she said, "I would be glad to start today."

Mrs. Juvland raised her eyebrow. She held up the reference in her hand. "Well, I was hoping to make a couple of quick calls about this first. Just formalities. But this weekend would be marvelous."

Ruth fidgeted with the hemline on her dress. "But, you were happy with it?"

"Oh, yes," Mrs. Juvland said. "Dr. Banker seems to think the world of you. And if everything he says is true then. Well, we would be so happy to welcome you into the family."

Dr. Banker looked at his computer screen. He adjusted one of the wires that led into Ruth's circuitry. He typed a few lines of code and hit enter. Ruth's eyes opened.

"Ok, let's try this," Mr. Banker said. "Tell me how you feel about the children."

Ruth blinked a few times as the program booted. Then she said, "I love them very much."

Dr. Banker nodded. "Good." He made a note on his screen. He looked at Ruth again. "What is your first memory of them?"

Ruth's circuits whirred for a moment as she referenced the images in her mind. "I've always known them," she said. She looked at Dr. Banker. "Is that right?"

He smiled.

After she left the Juvland's house, Ruth walked to the bus slowly, a huge smile spreading across her face. She thought about the past months. About the many meetings with Dr. Banker. She remembered how, week after week, she had felt increasingly certain about the children. They appeared in her mind as absolutes. There never could be no children. During the few tests Dr. Banker ran when the children were temporarily taken from her, she had felt agony inside. She thought about the nurses in the care center who helped her with her programming medicine. How proud they would be of her when she told them about her conversation with Mrs. Juvland. How happy they would be to hear that she was finally being released to love the children!

She stood at the bus stop, staring at the sky, sure that there had never been a nicer day than this one.

Dr. Banker ran a few more scans. He adjusted a few sub-processes. He ran through a few of Ruth's antagonistic options to make sure she had a full-range of emotions available, but then set the main-frame back to normal.

"One more time," he said. "Tell me about the children."

Ruth blinked as the system processed. Then she smiled. "I love them," she said simply.

"Is that definite?" Dr. Banker said. "We can always try a few runs without them."

Ruth involuntarily shuddered. "Please, don't," she said. "Please. I'm so happy when they're with me."

Dr. Banker typed a few lines of code. "Alright," he said. "Let's try some security runs."

Suddenly awful scenarios appeared in Ruth's mind. Her senses were on high alert. Immediately a million test cases presented themselves to her. In a split second she internally failed to protect the children and her heart was shattered. Then, just as quickly, the same cases were repeated, and this time she was successful and saved them. The joy which flooded her was unbearably rich and sweet.

"How was that?" Dr. Banker said.

Ruth felt like she was breathing quickly though she knew that wasn't possible. "Good," she said. "Very hard. But so good."

On Saturday Mrs. Juvland helped her bring her suitcase up to the guest quarters. It was a room at the back of the house on the 2nd floor. Ruth looked around her as she walked up the stairs. The wall of the staircase was hung with photographs of the family. She saw the smiling faces of Mr. and Mrs. Juvland. She saw them in their wedding portrait. She saw them on a beach in Hawaii, long ago.

But, what truly caught Ruth's attention were the pictures of the children. The Juvlands had a boy and a girl. Mrs. Juvland told her Emma was 9 and James was 7.

"And, where are they?" Ruth said.

"They'll be home soon. Mr. Juvland is bringing them home from music practice now."

She opened the guest room door for Ruth and stood back, allowing her to look in for herself. The room was small, but spotlessly clean with a bed against the wall and a desk on the other side. Best of all, there was a window which looked out onto the back yard.

"Will it do?" Mrs. Juvland said.

"Oh, it's, it's perfect!" Ruth said.

Mrs. Juvland smiled. She began to tell Ruth some details about the house rules. Ruth allowed the words to drift by. her background systems picked it all up but forefront in her processes were the faces of the children she hadn't met yet. She felt the intense imprinted desire to love. To protect intensely.

There was the sound of a door opening from downstairs and Mrs. Juvland glanced down the hall. "That'll be the children now," she said. "Wait here. I'll get them."

She disappeared down the hall. Ruth continued to look out the window. She previewed possible scenarios using the digital representation of the children in her mind. She saw herself caring for them. She saw herself protecting them. She saw a million variations of herself saving them, from a tornado, from gunfire, from poisoning. She couldn't stop smiling.

Dr. Banker sat in front of Ruth. He ran her through a series of diagnostic tests. Her eyes tracked well. Her strength and speed were tempered to match her visual age, 18 years. He verified that she was artificially stunted from accidentally breaking something with her grip.

Finally, he sat back and looked at her for a long moment. He leaned forward.

"One more question," he said. "No tests this time. Just an answer. What if they were in danger?"

Ruth blinked. Her ducts activated and two saline drops ran down her cheek. "I would save them," she said. "Oh, it would feel so good to save them!"

Suddenly she heard the sound of excited feet. Ruth turned from the window and saw the girl and boy running up the hallway toward her. When they reached her door, they stopped and looked in at her expectantly.

"Hello," Ruth said.

The girl, Emma, glanced back down the hallway, as though looking for permission. Then she turned back and said, "You're quite young. Don't you think so, James?"

The boy smiled at Ruth and said nothing. Ruth knelt down in front of them. "Well, it's true, perhaps," she said. "I am 18, but that means I haven't yet forgotten how to play."

Both children smiled, in spite of themselves.

The first week flew by. Ruth spent every moment of the day with the children. She roused them in the morning and helped them dress. They had breakfast together and spent most of the morning in the garden. After lunch they played indoors, and Ruth taught them new games. In the hour before dinner she read to them. The only time she was alone was in the evenings after Mr. Juvland came home from work. Ruth sat alone in the kitchen while the family ate in the dining room. She could hear the children vying for Mr. Juvland's attention, chattering on about what happened that day.

In no time it was a full week already since Ruth had come to the Juvland's house. She lay on her bed at the end of the day, Saturday, and looked out the window at the shadows slowly lengthening across the back yard. She continued to previsualize every possible case when she might need to show love toward them, care for them, protect them. Her face felt like it was glowing with joy.

Soon her inner time registered night. So, she closed her eyes. But in her programmed dreams she continued to care for the children.

The next day in the garden the children were fussing with each other. James wanted the shovel. Emma refused him and continued to dig in the sand box.

"But, it's my turn!" James cried.

"Use a stick," Emma said.

"Please, Emma," James said, pulling on her arm. Emma was filling a pail with sand, each scoop going deeper into the hole she was making. James pulled harder on her arm, and the shovel suddenly came loose from the hole and struck him on his forehead.

James clutched his forehead in pain and began to howl. Ruth's care circuits lit up. She jumped up and cradled his head in her hands. He continued to sob, but Ruth made soothing noises and eventually his cry settled into a whimper. Ruth stood up and slowly led him back into the house.

In the bathroom she cleaned his forehead with a warm cloth. By then James had forgotten about the hurt, and his eyes were dancing, anxious to return to Emma outside. When he was finally clean Ruth let him go.

She heard him dash down the hall. Ruth washed out the cloth in the sink. She sat on the edge of the bathtub. Her inner wiring processed through a series of digital patterns. She felt the fading inner desire now that the danger pattern had evaporated. She smiled. She had saved him. Her circuitry buzzed with joy.

She allowed herself to imagine other variations on the same theme. Instantly she saw the shovel put out his eye. Then she saw the dirt infect a scratch on his knee. Then she saw the shovel miss him but saw him suffering from mental pain due to a psychological disruption in his relationship with Emma. Every situation flew through Ruth's mind. Finally, she quieted herself by replaying what had actually happened. She smiled as she re-experienced the joy she felt when she cared for him.

Briefly her sensors noted something new. The joy had been slightly greater in the moment when the incident happened. Ruth's circuits logged the results.

The next day Mrs. Juvland asked Ruth if she would accompany the children to music class. "It's just a few blocks over," she said. "I would take them myself, but I have a dentist appointment."

Ruth was overjoyed. She had not yet been outside of the house or garden with the children. She gaily helped them with their proper shoes and the three of them sang goodbyes to Mrs. Juvland as they walked out the front door.

They walked down the street together, Emma next to Ruth and James slightly farther ahead as he ran from tree to tree, banging on the bark with a stick. It was a fine day with the sun warming the tops of the trees, the dappled shadows moving gently across the yards of the neighboring houses they passed by.

Soon Emma found her own stick and was running after James, both children now tapping on trees and fences as they ran ahead. Ruth's eyes followed them.

As they approached the busy street ahead, Ruth suddenly felt circuits buzz with the knowledge of street danger. Every car that whirred past was replayed in her mind as a scenario: bearing down on a child, nearing a child, intending to strike a child. And every option replaced it with: Ruth pulling the child to safety, Ruth deflecting the car, Ruth covering the child her with her intensified arms. Several options presented themselves to her decision banks. Her program accepted every one. It felt wonderful.

They stopped at the crosswalk. As the children waited they danced from foot to foot, eager to cross. Ruth looked down at them with her sensors alive for any sudden movement which might put them too close to the street. She also previsualized every move she would make to protect them. Then, for a nanosecond, yesterday's new log from her scenario with James registered itself again.

Ruth looked up at the light. Her inner sequencing could tell it was about to turn red for the cars and then the pedestrian walkway would be green. A bird flew overhead. For the briefest of moments, she hesitated and then decided.

"Look, children," Ruth said, and pointed into the air. Both children looked up into the sky with their backs to the street. Ruth registered the flight angle of the bird. She noted where Emma was standing. Then she turned, and made sure to step just slightly in front of the girl, just enough to obscure Emma's vision of the bird. Emma took a step back to see more clearly, and then was falling into the street. Ruth turned and calculated the car's impact time. She delayed her response for the split-second it took her sensors to register complete danger for Emma, and then activated her program and swept the girl up into her arms and back onto the sidewalk. The car swerved, and the driver pulled over.

He opened his door and ran over to them. Emma was sobbing and James was white with fear.

"Is she okay?" the driver said, wringing his hands.

"She'll be fine," Ruth said, "There, there, dear girl. You're safe now." She kissed Emma's cheeks and stroked her hair. "It's okay now. You're safe."

Ruth beckoned to James. He ran to her. She held both children in her arms. Her sensors were alive with pleasure. More than she had ever felt.

That evening after Ruth read to the children she helped them with their pajamas. After the incident at the street corner Ruth had taken them to get ice cream, and, as she calculated, the children had soon forgotten what happened with the car and said nothing to their parents.

As the children were brushing their teeth Ruth continued to play back to herself what happened. She watched the bird fly. She anticipated Emma's movement. She calculated the angle she needed to slightly obscure Emma's vision. She watched the girl fall. Again and again she watched herself leap forward and save the girl. Each time she saved her the circuits in Ruth's mind accepted the memory and logged it. Eventually the pleasure she had felt died down into background noise as the registered memory became part of Ruth's low-level static. She frowned slightly. She ran through the memory several million more times. It was lifeless now. It held no spark.

After everyone in the house was asleep, Ruth quietly walked into the back yard. She stood for a few moments and allowed her programs to run. Instantly she rehearsed her entire life span. From the moment she had memory she had images of Emma and James in her mind. Though she hadn't been there, she saw herself witnessing their births. She watched them crawl for the first time. She heard their first words. It had all been supplied to the company by Mr. and Mrs. Juvland when they requested a model like Ruth. She had been given uploads of every home video and every still photograph. She was augmented with hours and hours of the Juvlands talking about their children, about their hopes and dreams for them.

Then, separately, Ruth ran through the entire library of possible variations on things with had never happened but might have. She saw complications in the births. She saw accidents which didn't happen but could have. She witnessed awful images of their imaginary deaths. She then heard Mr. and Mrs. Juvland talk about memories they had with their parents and wishes which never came true. She felt the ramifications of physical and psychic pain on Emma and James from tangible and psychological threats from any possible source.

Finally, Ruth instantly ran through every possible future scenario. Her quantum brain fulfilled the request and previsualized trillions of pathways. Ruth isolated the future moments when anything harmful might happen and again and again she allowed herself the programmed joy of round after round of successful protection.

When she was finished she stood quietly in the backyard and breathed in the night air. She evaluated her thoughts and was content with her decision.

She turned and walked to the garage. Her sensors picked up the smells of stale exhaust and turpentine. She sniffed again. Her circuitry registered the can of gasoline Mr. Juvland kept for the lawnmower.

Ruth picked up the can and walked back out into the yard. She looked up at the children's windows and imagined them safely sleeping in their beds. Carefully she poured the gasoline along the wall of the house. Once the boards were wet, Ruth took out a match. She lit it and held it just far enough away from the fumes so there was no contact. She breathed deeply. Then she flicked the match against the soaked boards.

Ruth's sensors lit up with the knowledge of the heat. She had waited until the match was flicked, but now she began to record her vision. She not only watched the flames blossom upward but also predicted their future paths. She previewed the flames successfully consuming the entire house. She was satisfied.

The fire quickly spread until the lower floor was completely engulfed in flames. Ruth's danger sensors were alive and pinging. She breathed in the feeling and felt her pleasure banks overflowing with radiating desire. The lights in the bedrooms went on. Ruth could hear Mrs. Juvland screaming. Then she could hear the children crying.

She danced up and down for a moment until she couldn't contain herself any more. Then she went in to save them.

Strawberry Skin

My wife has booked us an all-expense stay vacation for the weekend in the large hotel which overlooks the city. We have often looked admiringly at the hotel when we would take the occasional car ride around town. We choose this weekend because the hotel is next to a park where they will be having a harvest moon festival tomorrow night. When I woke up this morning I noticed a strange smell in the air. My wife said she didn't notice it.

She smiled and said, "Alice, you're a silly girl."

That must be true. I suppose I've known it my entire life. I have difficult times with people. I don't feel like myself around anyone except my wife. She has been patient with me since we went to a book club in college on our first date. Those kinds of occasions have always been difficult, but I went along this time because I liked this girl who had charmed me in the college bookstore the week before.

My wife is very patient with me, which is why I felt content to agree on this weekend together at the hotel. Because I only know her I will have complete control over who I spend my time with, something that makes weekends like this one easier. We're just coming down for breakfast on our first day when I see the strawberries. The breakfast buffet is spread out before us in the typical lavish style that becomes these kinds of hotels. There are pancakes, pastries, cold cuts, lots of fresh fruit, and strawberries.

My gaze feels unpleasantly pulled toward them. An empty plate dangles in my hand as I stare down at the berries' plump, ripe, red bodies. Each strawberry is dimpled throughout with tiny, minute indentations each containing a small black seed. I touch my temple lightly and twist my lips. It takes some effort, but I finally stop looking at them.

My wife and I sit at the table which faces the garden as we breakfast. She spends a lot of time talking about her upcoming meetings. I keep sniffing the air. There's definitely something there. She goes on for a while about mergers. She's tremendously important, and her confident manner of speech makes it easy for me to drift off without worrying too much about whether I need to answer her too specifically.

After talking about her meetings, my wife asks me how I feel after the week's-worth of new prescriptions. I haven't especially noticed a difference, but I want my wife to be pleased, so I go on in a breezy Mediterranean way about how much better I'm feeling. As I talk my mind slowly keeps returning to the breakfast spread with the strawberries. I don't feel quite right. In my thoughts the dimpled pattern of the strawberry skin keeps repeating itself…like it won't leave me alone. It seems so silly when I come right out and think about it, but I feel a slight yet definite degree of revulsion as I see those tiny, red, seeded dimples.

We return to our room. I ask my wife about the smell in the air. She brushes it aside again. Strange. She stares out the window for a while. I decide to take a jog. After pulling on my jogging gear I take the elevator to the ground floor. This hotel is nice enough to warrant hiring a man to open the door for the guests. I want him to know I appreciate him. I thank him for holding the door for me, but I purposefully avoid looking at the pattern on his tie.

I begin to jog down the sidewalk which borders the hotel. In a moment I am across the street and making my way at a brisk pace through the park next to the hotel. There is hardly anyone out today. The few people who I pass are all staring out blankly or looking up at the sky. I cross several thoroughfares and am just beginning to feel a degree of settled calm… when suddenly I come to a stop.

The path in front of me has been recently paved with fresh asphalt and the tar has gathered, while hardening, into a shallow collection of rippled waves near the edge of the sidewalk. I stare at the stippled surface of the black tar with a sensation reverberating through my mind. The asphalt ripples are regular but also unnatural and I can't explain to myself why I should hate looking at them. There is a faint shudder of revulsion in my mind. I breathe deeply several times while looking up at the sky. Everything about this feels so vividly familiar. The smell is stronger. It smells like freshly cut fruit with a hint of something fetid below it.

I return to the hotel. The rest of the day is filled with obvious activities designed to distract and placate. My wife and I take a moment together on the balcony. I don't remember much about what she says.

My wife leaves to make a phone call, but I stay on the balcony. I try to imagine what my life would be like if I was normal, if I had a regular job. But why bother. I know I couldn't manage it.

That evening in the hotel, before bed, I sit next to my suitcase and take out of a few of my things. I can't remember when I last used this case. It may have been last summer when I was upstate. As I remember the clinic I make a quick and easy decision to stop thinking about it. Instead I busy myself with my items and hands.

In order to most efficiently place my belongings neatly in a pattern next to me, I decide to kneel. The easy-swinging effort that is involved with removing each personal thing from the suitcase is pleasant, and I let myself gingerly slip into a pattern where each motion neatly bookends itself with the next one until I make a little game of it. This continues for a while until I can't quite remember what I was doing before I got here.

I decide to stand because that's the surest path of returning myself to a normal way of thinking, but that's when I suddenly realize that the pattern of the carpet has imbedded itself semi-permanently into the taut, red skin of my knees from the pressure of my kneeling body. I wish fervently that I hadn't kneeled for so long. The dimpled spots on my legs are so bright and so angry and no amount of rubbing seems to take them away. This won't do. Now it is very difficult for me to not think about the strawberries. I feel a definite and heavy stabbing enter my brain. It is like a deep, red scar. I feel sick, and I want to tear at my skin and claw at my eyes. That is precisely how I feel.

For a moment I picture myself living somewhere else. Somewhere far away where women fixed things in order to live. I imagine myself in some desert somewhere or in a war-torn town…walking home from the vegetable market with a basket of maize on my head. I am connected in some way to all of them. For a moment I pictured these women all turning to look at me. Their gaze was open and blameless. They were not judging. But they were not inviting either. My thoughts falter.

I began to take my medication shortly after walking in the park one day during our first year of marriage. The episode seems contained in my memory as a perfect encapsulation of my psyche. I had just entered the shadows of the trees in the park when I saw the broken crate.

I picked it up because it looked like the kind of thing I might have found in an antique store. I was about to toss it back when it occurred to me, I could probably fix it. It might be fun to try.

There was a faux quality to my life. What it made it worse, was that I knew it and accepted it. I regularly came home from trips to the mall with bowls I didn't need but which I had chosen because they belonged in the kind of kitchen that I wished I had. I often leafed through magazines and lingered over pictures of living rooms containing fireplaces assembled from massive, rough rocks and imagined how delighted I would be when my living room looked like that…all the while knowing those pictures contained lives I would never own.

I put the crate on the porch when I arrived home and then went into the garage. I grabbed a hammer and several nails and then set about hammering. In less than ten minutes I was done.

I couldn't believe it. I held it up and felt a strange glow of pleasure. It would make a nice centerpiece for the dinner party that night. My wife had talked me into agreeing to try a social occasion if it was in our house rather than in someone else's. Mark and Caroline Brink were coming over. They were university professors in the psychology department across town. They had plenty of opinions about what might help me.

I like them, but they are fancy. If the crate was on the center of the table it might catch Caroline's eye. I brought the crate inside.

What made me feel guilty was that my mother came from an older generation where it was frightfully common to have married early and to have an entire roster of children before the women were 30. Those women belonged to a different category of mother or wife. It must have required a great deal of mental effort and an abundance of silent suffering to produce a type of house and a kind of life which would someday be elevated to the status of authentic rustic chic by today's standards of interior design.

Later that afternoon when my wife arrived home I was in the middle of experimenting with the crate. It took me a moment to notice her, but when I did I held the crate up proudly, "Look what I did."

My wife came into the living room and took a good look. "Where did you find that?"

"The park. The bottom was broken, so I fixed it."

"*You* fixed it?"

I looked at her. "Yes. What's so wrong with that?"

She smiled, "Nothing. You're pretty tough, aren't you?"

That evening, after the Brinks arrived, my wife brought everyone into the living room. The crate was positioned in the middle of the table. Caroline was helping herself to some chicken when she noticed it.

"Look at that then!"

My wife was pouring wine for everyone and said, "Yes, Alice made that. It was broken and she fixed it."

"Aren't you sharp!" Caroline said.

I said, "Oh, posh. Snip snap. It did make me feel awfully queer though."

"Queer how?" Caroline asked.

"Oh, you know. In that European way. Whose is it? Why was it there? *Should* I have taken it?"

We sat down to dinner, and I was disappointed. I fully expected Caroline to carry on a bit more about the crate.

After the Brinks left I was cleaning up the table and I went to reach for the crate…but then I stopped. No. It wasn't right. The patterns in the wood. They stood out in unpleasant visual swirls and divots. How had I not noticed that before?

I went upstairs and as I was applying my face cream I turned herself around a few times in the mirror. My thin, boyish legs bothered me. I fell asleep thinking about other women in faraway lands. They walked across miles of desert. But the desert was wrong. It was pockmarked through and through with awful bumps and jagged swirls.

The next day I took the crate out to the porch and shook it out to get rid of all the crumbs. I began to think of all the women again. I saw the crate perched against shapely, wide hips. Then I imagined myself as someone might see me from an airplane, a waifish housewife standing in an average backyard.

I stumbled a bit as I turned. I didn't feel right. I closed my eyes and steadied myself with one hand on the side of the porch. Then I put the crate down and went inside.

What *had* I been thinking? I couldn't do this. I wasn't some woman who found things and then fixed them. That was good for others. I couldn't do that.

I stood up and walked back out to the porch. The crate was lying on its side where I had left it. I bent over and picked it up. I grabbed a book of matches from the kitchen and walked to the fireplace. After lighting a match and touching it to the paper on the grate I took the crate and placed it carefully on the flames. They slowly encircled the wood.

I stood up and went outside. I grabbed the garden shears. I resolved to never walk through that section of the park again. And certainly, I would never bring anything like that home again. I frowned as I snipped at the few weeds in the garden bed.

A moment later I sensed a faint smell of smoke. I turned around and saw that the house was already on fire.

There was quite a hubbub after that. Ambulances, firetrucks, neighbors looking in. I said very little to anyone. I only broke down good and hard once and that was when my wife came home from work. Then I started taking the pills.

That night in the hotel I sleep fitfully and repeatedly need to turn and readjust my body and tuck my head just so. This happens often enough that around three I am positively wide awake and staring off into the middle darkness of the room. I hear my wife's deep breaths next to me.

As I look into the darkness I feel almost as though it were waiting for me…the strawberry pattern from breakfast begins to creep inward from the peripheral parts of my vision. Although the room is completely dark, my mind creates the rhythmic, undulating, ceaseless hollows of the strawberry skin and each tiny, black dot at the shallow centers feels like it contains a black universe of unknown and unsleeping terror. I can't look away because now my eyes are closed and the pattern still hovers before my unseeing eyes.

The dark blackness of each dimpled strawberry spot seethes with a kind of distrustful spite, and I suspect there are wet places in there which contain eyes and clusters of things. I am embarrassed to be thinking this way, for I know I should not, and I have definitely not forgotten to take anything. I have followed the pill bottle instructions implicitly. Perhaps I'm dreaming. Surely this won't follow me into the next day.

Somehow, I sleep again and, in the morning, while I look up at the ceiling, I am relieved when I both see and feel a sense that the pattern before my vision has smoothed itself out again. The soft, off-white of the ceiling is mercifully free of any divots or crooked angles.

After the incident with our house we moved into a sensible apartment downtown. This time, with the benefit of the medication and the new surroundings I made a strong attempt to be good. I wanted to make a good impression on our new neighbors.

I liked thinking people notice me. I fancied that people's opinion of me was good. There were certain things I tried to do as I anticipated being watched. When I wheeled my trash can out on Thursday evenings, I always made sure the can was neatly pushed up against the curb. When I walked back toward the apartment building, I imagined someone had seen this and was impressed with me. "She cares," they must think.

When I ordered my coffee every morning, I made it a point to establish eye contact with the coffee shop employees. I smiled at them at all the right times. After stirring in my sugar, I folded the empty paper packets crisply and then I threw them in the appropriate, approved recycling container. I expected the baristas have noticed this. I wouldn't be surprised if when I entered the coffeeshop, each one of them might silently hope they would be given the chance to wait on me that day. They might even mention it to one another…like it's a playful game. I am different, and they've noticed.

When I filled up our car at the gas station I hoped someone noticed when I cleaned off my windshield. I pulled the squeegee in crisp strokes with just the right amount of pressure against the glass. Only a very talented person with a true care for humanity could manage her life and handle her car like I do. It takes effort to be the kind of person I am.

All of this in our new apartment life was fine and good, but the bird sounds were becoming more difficult to ignore. The apartment-building we lived in is old enough now for there to be the occasional loose fitting on the outer walls…and one of these fittings had slipped, creating a hole large enough for a bird to use. A bird did use it and now there was a nest behind the bookshelf in the guest bedroom.

This is what it looks like to be an upper-middle class citizen. We could afford to live in an apartment building that is considered quaint but which also has certain quirks. Our friends from the suburbs raved about where we lived. It made me feel good…important. But in order to have envious friends one needs to put up with life in an old building. This is the price one pays.

The initial bird was not an issue because it was quiet. It was after the eggs hatched, I realized I had a problem. This building had been built in the late 19th century the rooms had ornate shelves built into the walls…it was part of the place's charm. Because of this I couldn't just pull the bookshelf away from the wall in order to potentially free the birds or move the nest or do any other damned thing so that I wouldn't need to hear the chirps throughout the day.

The chirping always began around dawn. Because I sleep with a fan on in the background, for white noise, I didn't notice the chirping until I woke up and turned off the fan. Then I would hear it, like an itch under my skin. Suddenly I would be thinking about this unseen and disagreeable nest which was just inches from my interior life. I felt dirty.

I imagined the birds back there. Because I couldn't physically see them instead they took up a nest in my mind. They built their nest of dusty twigs and bits of string and yarn from around town. The nest in my mind took on a knotted, tangled quality. I couldn't stop thinking about it. Each time I heard the birds tweet I felt like they were going off in my brain.

Finally, I couldn't take it anymore. There was an old tool box left in our hall closet by the previous tenant. One morning when I turned off the fan and heard the first bird sound of the day I ran to the closet and threw out everything onto the floor where I could see the items clearly. The hammer did no good. I beat it against the wood of the bookshelf but only succeeded in creating several dents. Each time I struck the wood I thought perhaps the birds would fly away, but their tweets always returned and always in such a way that I heard them in my mind, nesting, feeding, bleating, crying, molting, shedding, covered with lice and filth and other awful things.

I returned to the pile of tools on the apartment floor and that's when I saw the skill saw. I plugged it into an electrical outlet next to the bookshelf and then stood on a chair so that I could get a better view of the upper sections of the shelves. I desperately tapped on the wood a few times, sort of like I was checking a melon for ripeness. I flicked the power switch on the saw. It blazed to life with a whirring blur. For a moment I forgot about the birds and looked at the fast-turning blade. As it rotated my mind felt finally at ease. I couldn't hear the sounds of the birds over the roar of the blade. It was mesmerizing. I held it in my right hand and slowly reached for the blade with my left. The initial blood didn't surprise me. It just felt warm. But I must have made a mistake for one of my fingers dropped away, striking the chair I was standing on and tumbling down to the floor. I felt the sting of the pain then, and let up on the power button. The saw stuttered to a halt and then I heard the birds again. Desperate for peace I lifted the saw and began to cut a slice of wood out of the upper shelf. Sawdust flew into the air and drifted around me.

In about a minute I had an opening large enough so I could peer behind the shelf. It was too dark to see anything. I ran back to the pile of tools and grabbed a small flashlight. I was careful to use my right hand as my left one was bleeding everywhere by now. I returned to the bookshelf and peered into the hall. Yes, I could see the nest. The mother was gone but there were several small birds, featherless, each raising a head above the rim of the nest in a rictus of hunger, each beak letting out a cloying screech. I reached into the hole with the flashlight and crushed the baby birds. When I pulled the flashlight out it was covered with blood and pieces of tiny beak. This fascinated and horrified me. I stumbled to my clothing closet, grabbed an old t-shirt, and stuffed up the hole I had cut.

That night we had friends coming to our apartment for dinner. The Brinks again. I had already anticipated what we might talk about and had mentally prepared several comments that were politically up to date. The Brinks would enjoy their time with me, I thought, and feel glad to have been invited. I might even tell them about certain parts of the bird story. Certain parts.

But that was before my wife arrived home, and soon it was clear there would be no guests. I broke down again in sobs and wails, and my wife held me and cradled me. I fell asleep while still laying in her lap.

The next morning, she suggested a clinic she had found online. I didn't want to go, but I felt I really had no choice.

I tell my wife I'm not hungry this morning and I go instead to the hotel gym. She is staring out the window again. Her head is turned away. I can't see her face.

I use my room key to let myself into the gym and the door closes behind me with the satisfying click of a well-manufactured piece of 21st

century architecture. There is so much joy within me at the door's shutting sound that I open and shut the door again twice more just for the pleasure that accompanies the crisp, snapping efficiency of the latch and strike plate. The lock is firm and reliable. It is not organic and there is no part of its surface which is fleshy or fungal or horribly cellular. I use the fourth machine from the door. Far enough away to be cautious…not the third one because that is an odd number and why bother?

I press the start button on the machine and there is a faint whirring sound which gently ramps up as the rotating band of the running track begins to turn. For a moment I stand still, feet on either side of the moving band, allowing my eyes to get lost in the blur of the spinning rubber surface beneath me. For a moment I fancy that I could stay here forever. Yes, I'm sure I could. And if I did, nothing would ever send me into a frenzy ever again. I want to stay here forever. I wish to stay here forever. As long as the band keeps turning beneath me and pulls my eyes along with it I will be safe and mercifully sound. But I mustn't stay here forever. People will wonder. My wife will find me. Then it'll be the clinic again, and I'll not return there.

Reluctantly, I break away from the moving band and settle into my run. The first ten minutes I gradually work my way into a rhythm that is fast enough to draw sweat. At long last something begins to feel right inside of me. My deep breaths feel cleansing and I can almost believe my last month was the life of some other girl who had some other pains, none of which I have or have ever had. I need not have worried.

Each step is firm. Every foot plant is sure. Every surface is solid. Each substance is clear. There are no strawberries.

I run for 20 more minutes until I feel my legs begin to complain and then I push the emergency stop button on the machine. The belt gradually slows enough to allow me to move into a walking pattern and I am almost unbearably grateful for the smooth rubber tread which crisply grips the soles of my running shoes.

The doctors warned me about mixing certain things with the pills. I didn't want them to worry, so I spent a good deal of time nodding. I didn't take them terribly seriously, though. That was before last summer.

Last summer we visited my wife's mother. My wife drove. She pulled the car into the driveway. It's my wife's mother's house. Her mother was having a party for the people who work for her.

We rang the doorbell and her mother opened the door.

"Come in, then," she said. She'd been drinking some. She put a spatula in my hand and told me to help with the grill out back. My wife told me she could handle the bags. I walked out back and started flipping burgers with my good hand.

It was a hot evening. The grill made where I stood hotter. Each time I flipped a burger my skin felt singed. It felt good, though, because my skin didn't want to pucker. It felt smooth and even. Sweat gathered by my temples and under my arms.

It was a big party. There were people indoors and out. Most people were drinking. There were bottles and cans everywhere.

Drinking was one thing the doctors warned me away from. But my wife was upstairs. I flipped the burgers, thinking. The downstairs fridge was just inside the door from the grill. I slipped inside, looking for a bathroom.

A week passed. I was out back, looking at the lake. The air was heavy and thick. I was wearing my swim suit. I didn't like standing on the lake shore because there were too many pebbles. They made awful dents in the bottoms of my feet. In order to stop thinking those thoughts I made up a game. I jumped into the water and tried to jump farther each time.

I played a few rounds. Each time I climbed out I brushed away mosquitos. One of them found a place on my ankle. I scratched at the bite.

After I jumped for a while, I squinted out at the lake. There was a small island out in the cove.

I started swimming. The water was warm like a bath. Some of it sloshed sloppily into my mouth.

I got to the island and sat in the shallow water. Small waves swept up against my wet suit, sucking the fabric against my skin.

I swam back. That night when my wife was asleep I went downstairs.

Another week passed. I was out at the water again. The mosquito bites on my legs were itching me, and I scratched them hard even though someone told me that doesn't help. I hated the angry, red welts which rose from the scratching, so I scratched some more until I had some blood coming which covered the bites.

I jumped into the water and started to pull. The water was warmer. Someone said it didn't fully cool down there until November.

I got to the island and sat in the shallows again. The water lapped against my legs while I absently brushed at the mosquitos.

Soon it was a month. My body was slack and sallow, especially in the evenings. One day I didn't know where my wife was. I put on my swimming suit and went down to the lake.

The water was dead still. The sun on it hurt my eyes. I squinted out at the island. I jumped up and down a few times. I ran and jumped into the water and let my body sink all the way down to the muck below. The water down there was cool. I let my feet sink into the slime at the bottom of the lake. It was easier to stay down there, away from the hot sun and light.

I floated back up to the warm surface. I got out and jumped several more times, each time feeling my skin in my face move with the air, loose and lank. I felt the liquid in my stomach slosh every time I jumped. Finally, exhausted, I stood by the shore, my feet covered with mosquitos, more and more arriving all the time.

I jumped in one more time and started to swim toward the island alone. I didn't remember arriving there. My wife had to tell me later she went half mad with worry. She called all of her mother's neighbors. One of them said he saw me swimming for the island. My wife called 911.

By the time they got to me I was passed out. My body was covered with mosquitos.

I flick the button on the treadmill machine so I can walk some. The band slows to a gentle crawl. I take several firm steps. I love the feeling of the rhythm in my hips. I should say how utterly calm I finally feel. There is no concern within me.

I fantasize about what I might do next. First a good wiping with a towel. Then, perhaps the pool. The thought of the blue lagoon quality of the chlorinated water fills me with a sense of hope, and I really can't remember when I felt so good. After the pool I might sit for a spell in the sauna. If I stayed in there for at least thirty minutes then I might be able to work up a sweat which would be enough to take out of my skin all worry of dents or small imperfections. I smile to myself. I almost laugh with joy.

After the machine has completely stopped I turn to the door to leave…and that's when it strikes me. I smell something in the air…which I know is not really there…and I hear, yes, yes, I hear music although I know there are no sounds. I drop my towel to the floor and, sure enough, just like last time, the floor begins to tilt and sway, and the mirrored reflections of myself which I see in all corners of the gym are suddenly spinning. There is a horrible rippling insect darkness which spreads inward, closing around my mind like a drain.

There is a yawning chasm into which I am falling. I look up and I see the fitness room in the hotel flying far away from me above until nothing is left except a tiny bright star in the universe of blackness that surrounds me. Except, sure enough, the universe around me isn't quite black…not entirely. It has embedded into its fabric a million, billion microscopic divots and pinpricks and pores and glands. They pulse as though they were gorged with thick, angry liquid and they change with an uneven regularity so that, the moment I think I see them clearly, they have already changed into another pattern, each pattern moving against itself, up and down and from side to side.

The knowledge that this pattern has completely surrounded me in this black state of unconsciousness makes me start to suffocate…yet, I cannot escape. There is a gravity somewhere that won't let me go and is pulling me irretrievably downward toward some seedbed of sickness far below. And somewhere down there below me I hear a steady thrumming churn, like something being digested in acid. If only I could wake up, oh, if only the horrible, sliding, black, undulating, permeable pattern would release me, yet it doesn't, and I fall and I fall until I see an eye opening below me in the darkness that has within it the scarred history of countless universes of blistered, bulbous, leprous skin. I open my mouth to scream, but, as is true of dreams, no sound comes. The eye below grows wider and wider. It wants to swallow me. It wants to sew me into itself. It wants my strawberry skin.

I hear sounds. I am awake. I believe I am on the ground. I can't tell. There is something covering my eyes. Perhaps a blindfold? I hear voices. They are all the voices of people who must have found me…where? Oh, yes, here in the gym. On the floor.

The voices are encouraging and worried and one young female voice presses her hand firmly against my shoulder as I try to rise. She tells me to lay still…the ambulance is on its way.

The next several sounds are difficult to clearly remember. I hear an ambulance. I hear the crisp clicks of a stretcher being opened. I hear the vehicle driving. I hear kind voices again.

The ambulance stops. I feel myself being whisked inside somewhere. It feels cool inside. I am so relieved. I picture in my mind's vision an absolutely endless tapestry of white hospital sheets stretching as far as the horizon of my mind and they are all completely and flawlessly sharp and smooth and absolutely unwrinkled. They say I must wear the blindfold. It will help me heal.

Oh joy, they have given me something for sleep. I sleep in total darkness with the solid weight of the dear earth pulling me down securely against my bed. The darkness is total and complete with no seams and with only the reassuring embrace of black comfort.

The next morning, I awake. Refreshed. I am still blindfolded. For a few moments I lift my hands above the bed and wave them through the beautifully cool air of the hospital room which surrounds me. There is a quiet buzz somewhere behind the walls which gives me the sense of fine-tuned machinery and of gears and wheels which fit into each other perfectly and spin just right. Everything is fine.

I hear my wife's voice as she comes into the room. She tells me they are going to remove the blindfold. Slowly it comes off. My eyes adjust. My wife asks how I feel. I look at her. I scream. I scream and scream. On her face and skin there are strawberries.

Lidérc

The two holy men traveled by day, each of them on their own mule, riding slowly through the grass, until they came to the cabin in the valley. It was not marked on any maps.

The older priest, Father Janos, had been given care of the small gathering of villages in the north mountains. He intended to stay among the villagers through the winter and tend to their needs. His younger protégé, Gabor, had only done church-work in the city and never been to the mountains. "You'll never meet the people's needs if you don't travel the land," Father Janos told him. "The people in the mountains are poor, but they have lives and burdens of their own. Sometimes a single visit can give them a taste of hope."

He invited his younger protégé, Gabor, to accompany him. Long days and nights of travel wear on the minds of the best of men. Conversation between the two friends over the campfires brought their minds closer together. Gabor watched the older man throughout the day as they rode. He saw the aches and pains that accompanied old age, but he also heard no complaints from the grey priest. Father Janos, in turn, took moments from time to time on the path to talk about his life of devotion. He wanted to give his younger friend a glimpse at lessons which couldn't be learned in the bustling rush of the city. Plus, Father Janos expected he would be retiring in the next year or so and, when he did, he hoped Gabor might take over his parishes for him. This was the sure and certain way to broaden Gabor's vision for the world.

When they finally reached the cabin the afternoon sun was low in the sky and slanting rays caused splaying shadows to crawl across the grasses. The distant peaks of the mountains in the north turned purple in the twilight. The older priest was about to pronounce the time make camp when his younger partner motioned with his finger at a curling of smoke from behind the next ridge. They crested the grassy dune and through a strange wavering in the twilight air the small cabin came into view. The yard around the cabin was muddy and squalid and a general air of neglect hung over the sodden scene. Father Janos felt an eerie nudge enter his mind, but he pushed the thought away. It was late and they were both tired and in need of rest.

He dismounted and handed the bridle to Gabor. The young man brought the mules to the water trough, and Father Janos walked toward the cabin. His suspicion sharpened. There was no sense of life in the place.

There were no friendly stratchings of chickens or, indeed, of any other lively farm creatures. As he walked across the yard an unsettled sense of darkness entered his mind. His eyes were on the ground when he heard the cabin's door creak. He looked up. A figure stood in the darkness of the cabin's interior. Father Janos shielded his eyes from the slanting sunlight. Later he would say the deep scar on the man's face seemed carved deep enough to touch the its skull. The gash was crusted and partly healed by a scab of dark red blood. The rest of the man's facial skin looked mottled, as though he were fighting off some kind of infection brewing below the surface. Father Janos wished they had not stopped.

"Who are you?" the scarred man said.

"Travelers, sir. Bound for the mountain villages. Could we stay the night?"

The man stood in the doorway without moving. A low whine came off of the darkening lowlands as a wind storm circled slowly on the horizon. Then the man stepped back and shoved the door open with his boot. Father Janos hesitated. The cabin's interior was black. The hairs on his neck stood as he heard the wind whine through the slats in the walls. It was an ill sound and he wished to be gone from here. He was about to turn back toward the mules, when his young partner arrived from the water trough.

The scarred man disappeared into the gloom of the cabin. Father Janos followed after him slowly. As he stepped across the threshold of the hut the wind of the outside died and a dead stillness filled his ears. The atmosphere in the cabin was close and hot. The cabin had no windows, only four rough walls. Father Janos waited for his eyes to adjust, and then his heart skipped in his chest. There was another figure in the cabin. A young woman stood against the back wall where a stove puffed oily smoke against the low ceiling. The smell in the cabin was unrelenting, the acid tang of strong, wet manure.

"Stand in from the door," the scarred man said from a corner in the back where he stood. Father Janos strained to see him, but the scarred man kept his face turned away from the light. The pocket of darkness in which he stood seemed to conceal him like black soil.

The priest was about to step in from the doorway, but as he did, the young woman slid between him and the dark corner where the scarred man was. She had a blank look of fear on her face. She chanced a quick glance in scarred man's direction. His back was still turned. She threw back her head, exposing her white neck, and drew her fingers across her throat in a meaningful way. Her eyes were white and seemed half-crazed. Then she turned and disappeared back to the corner of the hut.

Father Janos quickly shoved his hand backward to stop Gabor from coming in any further. He took a step back and he chanced a quick look back at his young companion. Gabor's eyes widened in sudden understanding.

"Thank you anyway," Father Janos said loudly. "We'll try make the foothills by dawn." Without waiting for a response, he stepped out into the now complete twilight of the scrabbled yard and stepped quickly toward the water trough, pushing his young partner before him. His skin crawled with gooseflesh. He felt at any moment he might feel the clap of the scarred man's hand on his shoulder. He breathed a sigh of relief when they reached the trough.

They untied the mules who needed no prodding. They did not like this place. Their ears were flat against their heads and their eyes rolled back. No sooner had the men turned with their mules. when they heard the crunch of the scarred man's boot. Father Janos turned to face him. The scar was no longer visible in the darkness of the yard, instead there was a black void where the face should have been. Even through the wind the priests could smell him. It was the scent of a charnel house. Mold and dead meat. And below that something deeper and wet. Something imbedded within the thing's skin, encasing whatever it was in the shell of a man. Father Janos knew now it was not human. The smell from it caused a voice to sound in the priest's head. *Come closer. Come in here with us.* Father Janos actively fought against the voice in his head.

"Stay with us," the voice coming from the black void of the scarred man's face was low but it strangely carried in the stiff wind. It was as though there were two voices in it. One low and one high, like a whining child's. The voice was difficult to resist. Father Janos took a deep breath and reached into his robe to pull out the cross from below his shirt. The metal on the cross caught the last vestiges of twilight and the light played across the ground and flints of brightness danced between them. The scarred thing stepped back from the dancing beams of light.

"No, we'll continue on," Father Janos said. A moment passed. He felt the nervous nuzzling of his mule's nose against his hand. Then, without giving the being time to move, he swung onto his mule and turned out of the yard.

The two men rode their mules up to the crest of the hill before Father Janos looked back. By then the darkness in the sky had obliterated any shapes from the low valley and all he saw behind them was a bowl of darkness among the grasses.

They rode quickly across the first few hills and did not slow until several miles had been crossed and a cold rain was falling around them. Gabor was the first to speak.

"What was it?" Gabor said as he pulled up next to Father Janos.

"A lidérc," Father Janos said as he glanced back into the darkness. "Awful to leave the woman with it. It will be cruel to her for warning us."

They rode through the night. Occasionally they thought they heard a sound behind them, but nothing disturbed them in the dark. The mules plodded forward nervously and needed no prodding to keep up their speed. All around them the dark prairie breathed out the smell of night. They finally arrived at the village. Though it was still a few hours before dawn the innkeeper roused himself found them a room. They both slept fitfully and repeatedly Father Janos stood to check the dark hallway of the inn. He sensed the thing. It was coming.

***

In the morning Father Janos awoke and saw Gabor was already up. The older priest dressed quickly and found his young ward in the kitchen of the inn preparing breakfast. It was at that moment a young boy from the village came into the kitchen with a hurried step. He told them a woman had been found bleeding on the outskirts of the village. The boy said she begged to see the holy men. Father Janos hastened into his cloak and came out.

The boy brought them down to the village church where a number of the townspeople had gathered. The young woman was sitting on the floor between the pews. Her hair was so plastered with mud Father Janos hardly recognized her as the one from the cabin who saved them last night. A woman from the village coaxed her to drink some tea. Once she had caught her breath she unfolded her story.

She was originally from a village in the south. Her father was a farmer and she worked with him in the fields. One day two years ago she was tending the rows when the lidérc came upon her in the field. She was unable to resist it. She followed it into the woods. She awoke later in the thing's cabin. She was pregnant. It kept her tied to the bed through the weeks as her womb grew. The night she gave birth the creature hovered over her and quickly took the child.

Twice the cabin was visited by other travelers. Each time the lidérc coaxed them to stay the night and then murdered them as they slept. She didn't know what it did with the bodies, but it always disappeared the next day for many hours and when it returned its clothes were dark with the travelers' blood.

The thing had indeed treated her harshly after the priests left. It tied her to the cabin wall and whipped her. It was about to continue when the wind outside blew something against the cabin door and the lidérc went out to examine it. She was able to untie her hands and slip out the door before it returned. She fled toward the village on foot through the night, following the slow curves of the stream.

"I'm sorry," she said. "I may have led him here. I couldn't conceal my steps." Father Janos smiled and shook his head. "Thank God you are here," he said. When she finished her story, he sent Gabor around the village to bring the townspeople into the church. There were not more than fifteen of them, three poor farming families. They huddled against one another between the pews as the sun drifted between the clouds and unnatural shadows deepened across the sanctuary.

"It will likely come after sundown," Father Janos said to the people.

"What is it?" one of the men said.

Father Janos glanced at Gabor before answering. His young friend sat in the front pew with a barely concealed look of fear. "I've read about them, but never seen one before," he said. "Priests across the border talked about them being found in the higher mountains to the south. It contains within it a pool of darkness from below the mountains. The skin of its man-shape is what allows it to move around."

"What does it want?" a woman said. She pulled her children closer to her.

"It hears our blood," Father Janos said. "To the creature the blood is a drumbeat in our veins. They plant gardens of blood where they dwell below. And this one has a taste for it now. It is coming."

The townspeople's eyes were wide in fear. A small girl hid behind her mother's skirt.

"We have a chance," Father Janos said. "It can't ingest something which is consecrated. This is why it never eats the children. It only feeds on those old enough to have felt the turn of the earth." Father Janos stepped forward and looked at the small, huddled group before him. "To defeat it we must all work. Will you help me?"

The men looked at one another. Silent nods passed among them. A stout man stood forward from the rest and looked Father Janos in the eyes. "What must we do?" he said.

***

The dark creature streamed through the night. It paused from time to time to sniff the ground. Each time it did, the bright smell of the woman was stronger. It was as though her scent was a beam of red, flowing through the plains, twisting from hill to hill, growing richer all the time. It had been awhile since the creature had last fed and there was a powerful hunger growing within it. It had taken great effort to keep the woman but not to consume her. Somewhere in the creature's travels it had learned that if it maintained the shape of a man and had a woman living with it then travelers were more willing to stay for the night. This supplied the creature for many months with occasional visitors, but the priests had been the first travelers in a long while. As its hunger grew the skin it was wrapped in became thinner, threatening to allow the black pool within to spill out. Below the mountains the blackness could be contained by the layers of rock. Above ground it needed the human skin to remain strong if it wanted to breed and pass itself on.

By the time the creature saw the town ahead its lower jaw hung open and black saliva flowed out. Now the woman's scent mingled together with other shades of crimson. It sensed the other villagers. It smelled men and women. Different ages. Different lives. It felt a turn of hunger in its belly. The thing saw the lines of color all flowing together into the small church at the center of the village. It slowed its walk. The meeting with the priest in the cabin had made it cautious. The priest was different. He knew something of the earth and something of the soul the creature had not yet known.

It approached the door of the church. The beating of hearts inside the building was strong in its ears. The creature held out his hand and pushed the door open. Light from the sanctuary flowed out into the night. The thing stepped through the door.

The townspeople were all seated in the pews. Their backs were turned to the door. All eyes were on the front of the sanctuary where the older priest stood with his younger ward next to him. The two holy men were behind a low table, empty but for a single bowl.

The older priest held in his hands an open volume of scripture. He met the thing's eyes and for a moment they stared at each other. Then the priest looked down at the assembled crowd. He said, "The Lord be with you."

"And also with you," the assembly murmured together.

The thing sensed a faint trembling in the air. For a moment it hesitated. Then the priest took a knife from under his cloak and laid the blade against the skin of his forearm. As he said the next words he slowly cut across his wrist. Blood flowed down his hand and began to drip into the bowl.

"Lift up your hearts," the older man said.

"We lift them up," the crowd responded.

The creature's senses were inflamed by the scent and sight of the blood. The blazing light from the crimson drops completely absorbed its senses.

"Take this, all of you, and eat it," the priest said. "This is my body which is given up for you." The priest handed the knife to the younger priest. Then Father Janos began to remove his clothes. He folded each piece carefully and laid them to the right and left of the bloody bowl. As his skin was uncovered a howling hunger built up in the stomach of the creature.

"Take this, all of you, and drink from it," the priest spoke, with a shiver in his voice as the night air touched his skin. "This is the cup of my blood."

The priest removed his last item of clothing. He lifted his knee and carefully knelt onto the table. Then he fastened his eyes on the creature again. Then the priest took the knife into his hand again. "Do this in memory of me," he said, and he cut his throat.

Blood sprayed into the air. The priest's body fell to the side and the fountain of blood shot onto the back of the sanctuary and splattered the wooden crucifix. The sight and smell of the blood filled the eyes of the thing. With a single movement it crossed the space between itself and the priest's body and fell upon the bloody table with open jaws. In the last moment before the creature sank its teeth into the throat of the priest, the older man's eyes turned and he looked at his young ward in a meaningful way. Then the thing bit off the priest's head.

In the next moment a high-pitched shriek filled the church. The skin of the creature began to sizzle. A horrible smell of rot filled the air and was immediately replaced by the scent of burned hair. The people in the pews crouched down. The younger priest stepped back and picked up a bucket of holy water and threw the water across the jerking body of the creature. Streams of water mixed with blood poured off the table and flowed toward the pews. Outside of the church, forest creatures fled back into the woods as a burst of lightening from within the building flashed out through the stained-glass windows, turning the dark night outside into kaleidoscopes of color.

The young priest stepped forward to the table where the creature was writhing on the dead body of the older man. Gabor took the book into his hands and droplets of blood from the mangled body of the older priest splattered his face as he read, "Drink ye all of it; for this is my blood of the covenant, which is poured out for many." With each word spoken the creature's cries of pain rose until the piercing note seemed to shake the walls of the church. Mingled in its voice was the crowded sound of many harmonies of other voices within its skin. The voices rose and fell in a ghastly chorus. The townspeople crossed themselves and frantically poured out of the entrance of the building. Gabor was the last one out. He motioned to the men. They stepped forward and nailed boards across the door.

Inside the anguished cries of the creature began to weaken. The townspeople knelt on the ground outside. As the shriek from within died away the young priest continued to read from the book. Soon everyone else joined in: "Our father who art in heaven, hallowed be thy name…"

***

Dawn rose over the village. It was a Sunday in spring. What happened in the church months ago had changed the ground under the wooden structure of the building. The earth and stones were black as though burned and scarred. The pool of darkness which had been contained by the lidérc's skin had long ago seeped back into the earth, but its mark remained.

Slowly the people from the town rose from their beds. The men tended to the chores. Women prepared a morning meal. A few children ran through the streets. Then, as mid-morning drew near, the townspeople filed out of their homes and slowly congregated at the front door of the church.

Father Gabor opened the door and welcomed them. One by one the families entered the sanctuary. Friendly conversation flowed between the townspeople and the priest. After everyone was inside, the young man stood outside for a moment, soaking in the morning sun. Then he turned and looked up at the sign above the front entrance. The sign read, "The Church of Father Janos". The young priest smiled, turned, and entered the church.

.

One Particular Girl on a Stage

A hot planet orbits a sun. The planet's surface is angry with heat. There is a crowding of people below ground. There are cramped tunnels. There is a long line leading up to a stage. This line forms again every month. It must. One by one the people step onto the stage. The stage faces a massive crowd. And in the line is one particular girl.

I know I can't do this anymore. The line inches forward. People, one by one, take their place on stage. It will be my turn soon. What will I say this time? Nervously I look down at my hands. I hold my book.

A man ahead of me steps up to the microphone. The massive crowd is quiet. He lifts his carbon filter and says into the microphone, "mother". There is a whispered murmur in the audience, and he leaves the stage. To calm myself I flick the book in my hand to a random page and read silently to myself, *"How long shall I cry for help?"*

***

I have lived in New Toronto for 10 years. I live in a warren-like structure buried two stories below the earth. It is still possible down here to regulate the temperature from the scorching, ever-increasing heat above ground. Now the only people who go above ground are those wearing the cooling suits. These underground mazes are standard in New Toronto now. The only places still cool enough to live above ground are far, far to the north.

My family immigrated here from Mexico voluntarily. Voluntarily is no longer how people arrive here now. Now people *must* come here. The places down south are too hot. For a while people had naturally been drawn either to Europe or to North America. People came north looking for a cooler climate, because it just felt better. Eventually it was no longer a matter of choice. The screens call this new immigration mode "unsolicited global transfer." The news arrives on the screens constantly. The screens occupied every square foot of the walls down here. All the walls. All the halls. All the rooms. Screens everywhere. There is hardly any paper anymore. Screens could be kept cool. Paper was dangerous. Paper had been off-limits since 2025. Manufacturing it caused too much heat. And above ground it might ignite accidentally.

I remember my mother telling me about her favorite books from when she was a little girl. We had a library in our apartment in Argentina. My mother was a teacher and she collected books. She sometimes showed me new ones she had bought. She said, "Look at this one, Lula. And look at this one. Someday, this collection of books will be yours." But it won't be. That collection, that library, those memories…they have all burned.

* * *

I look down at the book in my hand. The one book my mother managed to bring with us on our journey north. It is a relic of a world long gone. I don't usually bring it with me to the monthly Speaking Bee, but for some reason I grabbed it today.

The next person in line for the microphone is a young girl, probably 12 or 13…my age. Her hair looks like mine except more blond. Mine is in a pony tail while hers is in braids. She also looks awake. It is more and more rare to see young people alert. Most parents have begun to dose their children with alcohol throughout the day. This calms them down and makes their energy easier to contain. This new life below ground has probably been hardest on the children. Adults could see this future coming from miles away. They also understand the rules and why. Children still want to run. They still want to laugh out loud and scream and cry and talk with their friends. All of those things are illegal now.

As the girl walks forward, I grip my book tightly against my chest. I am trying to decide what word I should say when it's my turn. There are a few words that I have already nixed like, "Air-conditioning" and "summertime." The rules are strict. You are allowed one word…two syllables. Anything longer takes too much time to say and releases too much carbon dioxide. Anything shorter than two syllables doesn't do enough to exercise the vocal cords and that could cause atrophy and other problems down the road. The rules are intentional. Two syllables. No more. No less.

The young girl raises her filter and says, "chocolate ice cream". There is a loud buzzer. The guards take her arms and replace her facial carbon filter. She is taken backstage. I know she wouldn't be back for two months and then she will definitely be medicated. At the Speaking Bees there are almost always one or two children to make the syllable mistake. The adults all get it right. Well, everyone who isn't trying to get shot. The adults all rattle through predictable words which all sound vaguely similar and all form the never-ending monotony of my life beneath the ground. As

I stand in these rows every month, I hear a litany of different words rolling from the loud-speakers. Candy, tulips, swimming, sunshine, Christmas, and on and on. All memories of things now lost. I still haven't decided what I'm going to say today. Nervously I glance behind me and flick to another random page in my book. I lower my eyes and read, "...*eternal chains under gloomy darkness...*"

***

It isn't hard to remember how things got to this point. We are bombarded by safety announcements and reminders. The screens all around us constantly play the safety videos. On the videos Mrs. Manners' smiling face chatters on and on about safety steps and what to do if we feel the air around us getting too hot. The matron minders who give us our pills every day are required to restate the facts to us every morning, noon, and night and now the whole scenario just runs on autoplay through my head all the time. The screens continually repeat the history of the world, making sure no one can take a single step without remembering how we got here. I suppose it is meant to keep us vigilant. The government requires this kind of constant repetition because the situation above ground has become so precarious. They want no mistakes. The planet's future hangs on a slim thread, and at any moment that thread might ignite.

Mrs. Manners is a digital creation of the government. Her face on the screens always smiles. She's always perky. She makes daily announcements. She is somewhere on every screen. It's almost like she's a voice in our heads, constantly reminding us to make the right decisions and take the right steps. It's like she's been branded into my retina and burned into my ears. Everywhere I look I can see and hear her.

She's a big part of the safety videos. The safety videos repeat the story day after day. Sometime during the first days of the last century, the world was finally scorched beyond repair and left barren and raw except in a few northern reaches. The global drumbeat of warning against a warming planet finally took on an undeniably urgency when several flash incidents of spontaneous atmospheric combustion happened over some of the larger cities in the danger heat zones. Those tropical regions were always warm, but nothing like this.

People down there would cultivate rice in wet fields. The rice pickers would move from row to row, harvesting in a rhythm which matched the earth's seasons. Slums surrounded large cities. The rich lived in the city. The poor were in the slums. The seasons came and went. That world is gone. There are no seasons anymore. Just heat. The rice pickers are gone. The fields are parched and dry.

Around the planet's middle belt, the cities began to ignite. New Delhi, during a particularly bad spell of air pollution, experienced a city-wide ignition event and was instantly vaporized in a wave of searing flame. The pollution in the atmosphere above the city reached just the right degree of heat and the chemicals in the air had just the right combination to achieve fire. It happened so quickly and with such a massive explosion that the waves in the atmosphere crossed the globe three times. The screen reporters compared it to the Krakatoa volcano eruption centuries ago.

After New Delhi was gone it was as though the earth had developed a taste for ridding itself of dangerous, overpopulated hotspots. Several other Indian cities burned themselves out of existence in the next few days. Mumbai, Hyderabad, Jaipur. All gone and nothing left in their place but black scorching and a kind of primitive covering of spontaneously created glass. Then some cities farther north began to go. Istanbul suffered from a magma-infused earthquake far below the surface of the city and simply slid off the continental shelf and into the sea, half of it disappearing into the Black Sea and half into the Mediterranean. A moment of poetic irony perhaps for a metropolis which so long linked the earth's regions of Asia and Europe.

Soon other cities in the hot zone around the earth's middle ignited. Cairo, Mexico City, Jakarta. An uninhabitable swath of heat began to creep north and south from the equator, and that is when the global migration became frantic. It was as though the earth was loosening its belt after a long meal and not containing itself anymore. People were frightened. It turns out it is one thing to warn people something bad is going to happen if they don't change their lifestyle. It's something quite different when you realize your city's weather forecast is approaching 115 degrees with an air pollution index of over 800, and you know this means only a single spark is necessary to create another New Delhi.

The daily safety videos rattle through this history on the screens, hour after hour. While the ignitions were happening around the middle of the planet, the rise in the earth's temperature melted the ice on the north and south poles. New Delhi's burning and the heat of the similar cities in its wake caused things to speed up and warm up considerably worldwide. Within a few weeks the Arctic Ocean had shrunk by half. Antarctica by three fourths. And something else happened which the scientists hadn't anticipated. There were subatomic particles frozen deep within the ice of Antarctica which began to enter the earth's atmosphere. These particles had been frozen and dormant since the last ice age. Once these tiny whirling molecules began to spread around the earth the scientists were able to get a look at them for the first time and they realized, with dread, what they were. These were a kind of planetary immune system. Just as the human body floods itself with chemical healing agents when a fever develops, it turns out the earth had something similar up its sleeve. These particular molecules had an ignition level within them which corresponded to the rising temperature of the earth. I imagined them as tiny sparks now rife throughout every square centimeter of the air just waiting to catch the right circulation of downdrafts and atmospheric mixing to generate a small flame…and then…boom. These subatomic particles seemed programmed to speed up the warming process with a kind of intentional design, accelerating the earth to the point where it could rid itself of what was causing the heat: people.

Things began to happen very quickly. The oceans rose. People fled inland and northward. Deserts spread. Soon Africa was nothing but one solid field of sand…and the sand in its exact middle was so hot from the atmospheric condition and the rays of the sun acting like a magnifying glass from the silica all around it that it formed at the center of the continent a massive, swirling pool of scintillating, undulating liquid glass. The glass reflected the sun and this caused the temperature to spike higher, as though Africa was an eager boy scout holding a mirror and a magnifying glass and channeling the sun's rays onto a planetary campfire. The Atacama Desert in Northern Chile advanced down the slopes of the Andes so quickly people later claimed they could see it moving if they watched it for more than a few minutes. They said it was like a pulsating ocean of inhuman beachfront, creeping towards the outer edges of the South American continent like a wide, open, dry mouth. It acted as though it was alive and chewing. Perhaps it was.

Soon every place in the southern hemisphere was uninhabitable. The last animals on earth disappeared. Some died. Others ran off into the wilderness. The people continued to hurry north. The last flights of environmental refugees took off from the airports in Sidney just days before the vast interior of Australia finally claimed the remaining population centers along its coasts. Tasmania lost its subterranean grip on the continental shelf beneath its landmass below the waters and shifted northward, drifting along the eastern side of Australia. It broke apart as it slowly curled northward and completely destroyed the Great Barrier Reef.

After the Gobi Desert had shifted to cover most of northern China and to the west across Eurasia, the only sustainable population centers were on either side of the Atlantic. The earth was uninhabitable below the 38th parallel. Most island cities were under water. Singapore was gone. The Pacific Ocean had grown to two thirds of its original size, swallowing up land on both of its coasts far inland and far up the sides of mountain ranges. The volcanos across Indonesia began to erupt and reshape the earth's crust, lowering that country's 17,000 islands below the surface of the expanding ocean. The effect of so much landmass disappearing below the surface of the water served to only accelerate the water's rise in other parts of the world, the same way a bath rises when someone sits down into it. In this case, the earth was tired of the eons of misuse and damage and had decided to lower itself back into the submerged depths and wait for things to get better. Temperatures continued to rise and creep northward. Finally, a few sparse locations in Europe and America were the last global locations where the temperature was mild enough for people to live. And people flocked there like frightened animals leaving a burning forest.

***

Another repeat of safety videos just finished on the screens around me. I can hear the history echoing in my ears. The line ahead of me in the Speaking Bee moves forward again. The next person in line is a little boy, maybe 5 years old. He struggles to pull down his mask as he reaches the microphone. A matron minder steps forward to help him. He's so short that the minder lowers the microphone to his level. The boy automatically smiles at the minder, and says, "Thank you, madam." There's a gasp from the audience and immediately the buzzer sounds again. Too bad, kid. Four-syllables. Too much time used. Too many sounds. Too much CO_2. No grace for mistakes. The guards come forward, replace his filter, and he's gone. Hopefully he won't make the same mistake next time.

What will I say when it's my turn? Since my nightmare last night, I've had plenty of time to think. I've been awake since 3AM. My dream is still branded into my memory, like a fiery wound. It's hard to summon much enthusiasm for a process that seems doomed, but we have to be here. Anyone absent is immediately found and put on an extra dosage of pills. The Speaking Bees must go on. I nervously pull my book out and leaf through the pages again. My eyes fall on a fresh passage, "*Let the day perish on which I was born…*"

***

I remember going to school in Argentina before my family ended up here. Our life was simple. Father, mother, and me. In my class the teachers taught us regular subjects. There were no constant warning videos. We learned about famous writers. We read books. We learned about famous catastrophes from centuries past. Names like Fukushima, Katrina, Chernobyl, and Moscow. Back then I wouldn't have believed that I would someday be living through a global catastrophe myself. As is true of all catastrophes, this worldwide heat catastrophe hadn't been planned…but it could have been anticipated. There had been a steady drumbeat of warning signs and fearful predictions during the years leading up to the mass exodus away from the hot zones. The safety videos on the screens around me keep reminding us of the steps which should have been taken.

The world government had clearly not anticipated the problems involved with having the world population concentrated so tightly in just two northern locations: Ireland and central Canada. I don't remember who coined the term, but, at some point, the news was alive and vibrating with the new phrase "terminal atmospheric carbon vortex." It had not been anticipated that having so many people living and speaking and breathing in two concentrated global areas would cause the carbon dioxide problem in the atmosphere above the North Atlantic. There were now two ozone holes in the atmosphere hovering high above the earth, each letting in a higher and higher concentration of UVB. The ozone holes were like two nostrils on the earth's nose and it was inhaling heat from the sun faster and faster every day.

In retrospect it makes sense. There were over 25 billion people living in two areas that were both smaller than the size of Great Britain. That meant a lot of mouths breathing out a lot of carbon dioxide all day and all night. The carbon dioxide swirled up into the atmosphere above Ireland and Canada and, voila, the ozone holes formed. The earth seemed to have developed a taste for ridding itself of irritants by now. Warmth that had normally taken centuries to develop was now accelerating year by year in leaps rather than creeps. The remaining world leadership decided the population needed constant, rigorous, unceasing daily reminders about the need for vigilance against any possible further carbon dioxide contamination of the atmosphere. This meant my life was dominated day in and day out, hour by hour, sometimes every few minutes, with reminders and coaxings and threats to make sure I never forgot how we all got here.

In addition to the matron minder teachings every week, viewing the short education video was also part of the daily regimen of required information. That's why the screens were everywhere. A new mandate required that no one be able to go anywhere without being within viewing range of a screen. And the screens all showed the same thing, 24 hours a day.

One safety film showed cartoon images of people living in Northern Europe and Canada, and it showed us breathing out massive amounts of carbon dioxide. Then a cartoon version of a huge swirling hurricane developed above the heads of the cartoon people and suddenly two massive holes like crooked scars opened in the upper atmosphere of the planet. Cartoon lightning bolts of sunshine entered through the scars and the cartoon people down below stopped speaking and started to fan themselves nervously. Finally, the smiling face of Mrs. Manners appeared. She held her finger up to her mouth and said, "From now on… Shhhh!" And then she held up the now familiar device. The government called them "self-regulating single-user carbon inhibitors." What they did was keep us from speaking.

Speech involves the exhalation of air. The average human body breaths out 500 liters of carbon dioxide every day. Lots of speaking can up that level to 600 liters. Speaking angrily and incessantly can easily make that 700. The government realized they had a lifeline on their hands. If speaking could be stopped, or drastically cut down, the level of CO_2 in the atmosphere might stabilize. Or maybe it was just another way of trying to appease the churning anger in the bowels of Mother Earth. Either way, the decision was made. People had to wear masks all the time. And no one was allowed to speak without them. Daytime and night. Normal food was virtually nonexistent anymore so that wasn't a problem. The masks had feeding tubes built into them so three times a day we were all hooked up to a trough like a perverted reversed kind of milking machine.

The first few weeks with the masks had been very difficult. The facial masks were large and cumbersome. They each contained a whirring mechanism which cleaned every breath of air, reducing the amount of CO_2 ultimately emitted to .002 percent. The masks closed incredibly tightly and the seal gripped the skin so much that most people smeared their faces with Vaseline before putting them on. The claustrophobia was made worse by the heat. When mother first put the mask over my face I thought I would suffocate. It took a great deal of concentration to prevent panic. But that was also the point. The facial carbon filters in the masks forced slow breaths so that only careful, methodical movement was possible by design, slow movement and no speaking. I grew accustomed to slowing my breathing to long, deep breaths and slowing my walking to slow, lumbering, careful steps.

The screens all around us ran this reminder film, and several others like it, constantly day and night. Guards patrolled every inch of the rooms and hallways. If anyone tried to remove their mask, except during the Speaking Bees, those people were removed and most were never seen again. Everyone had masks. Everyone moved slowly. And everywhere from the screens Mrs. Manners smiled at us and said, "Shh…"

***

I've been daydreaming. I look up and realize there are only two people in the line ahead of me. Even though the Speaking Bees happen every four weeks, I still haven't really gotten used to it. Today is particularly awful because mother and father are no longer here. Usually I am with them, but last month my parents left for their scheduled work assignment in the north. My parents had been telling me that day would come. The same thing had already happened to most of the other parents of my fellow pupils. The pattern was dreary and familiar. The parents are gone one day, the matron minders begin to give an extra dose of pills each night, and soon the pupils seemed to stop caring.

At first, I couldn't understand how the pills could possibly make someone forget about their parents. There was a girl who slept in the bunk next to me. As parents of our fellow classmates began to disappear to places up north, we gradually saw more and more faces on the children around us grow slack and dull beneath the plastic masks. The girl next to me passed me a note one day.

It said, "Are your parents still here?"

I took out a pen and wrote, "Yes."

She wrote me back, "Mine left today."

I reached out and held her hand. Then I wrote, "I am sure they'll be back soon."

She looked at me and nodded. But, as usual, her pills were increased, and the next day when I passed her a new note she just looked at me with a vacant stare. I was horrified when I saw a thin strand of saliva creeping down from her lips beneath her mask.

As I step forward in line I can see the girl's face in my memory. I shudder. I take a deep breath to steady myself and open to a new page in my book, "*My strength was sapped as in the heat of summer.*"

The next person in line is a large man. He steps forward, takes a deep breath, and shouts a volley of obscenities. People in the audience immediately duck in practiced fashion and the rest of us in line automatically take two steps back quickly. The guards rush forward, and shoot the man through the heart. More and more people are doing this in the Speaking Bees. It's an easy way out.

***

The Speaking Bees were born out of necessity. The government said, "Stop speaking" and people did. People were quick learners, and, after Mrs. Manners in the video told us to be quiet, nobody used their vocal cords anymore. This immediately helped the carbon problem in the atmosphere, but it caused other problems. Apparently vocal cords can atrophy. The doctors had published several findings stating that if vocal cords weren't used at least once monthly then the corrosion of the diaphragm would follow. Sick people meant more hospital visits, which required extra venting, and that added carbon to the atmosphere. If sick people weren't helped then they died and dead bodies created methane. Methane rises and a hot earth, hoping to get hotter, loves methane. It's like a sip of hot tea on a scorching summer day. The government had to come up with a way for people to exercise their vocal cords briefly, in a controlled fashion.

Once a month in each ventilation district per underground housing unit people would line up, then wait, then step forward to the microphone, and then say one word, two syllables long. It needed to be an actual vocalized word. Just a random sound would not provide the vocal cords with enough activation.

The words also had to be said without the masks on. The masks gripped the skin so tightly they created a tiny atmosphere inside which was devoid of natural currents and molecules which the vocal cords needed. The doctors tried remedying this with pills, but, as it turns out, nothing replaces the natural environment of the earth for allowing life to live…whether it be for plants, animals, or vocal cords. So, the government decided that unless they wanted to do something drastic and exterminate most of the earth's population, they needed to figure out an organized way for people to exercise their vocal cords. The doctors determined that one word per month was enough. One word of vocal exercise in the open air and then there could be another four weeks of silence.

The question was, what word to use. Initially the government required everyone to say the same word because it could be more easily regulated. The word they chose was "transfix" because it used a wide range of sounds and vocal inflections. But then they realized the vocal cords needed more than just one possible pattern of repetition. So, people were allowed to choose their own words as long as they were different from last month and didn't repeat any of the same syllabic patterns. First people just said whatever word came to their mind, but over time people began to use their monthly words as a way to commemorate things which had been lost or left behind. People started saying things like "springtime" and "rainfall" and "smiling." All two syllable words. All things that people didn't have anymore.

One thing that made this pattern somewhat easier was the fact that English was now the universal language. The trend was already headed that way before the global migration north. Once everyone was living in Ireland or central Canada, the government took the final step and required the language patterns to be streamlined. Mrs. Manners still gave her instructions in English and Mandarin, but the Speaking Bees only allowed English words to be spoken. Not everybody liked this decision, of course. Inevitably some people decided to make their words more political...or spiritual. That's when the guards began to be used.

If anyone violated the rules the guards would detain them if the infraction was minor. People were taken somewhere, re-educated, and then brought back, usually under some kind of medication to make them more pliable. But more and more people were using their moment at the microphone to make a statement of some kind, and recently the guards had been authorized to kill if necessary.

***

The large man's body is cleared from the stage. The guards put his body into a self-sealing bag so that his emanations can be contained and then the body would be processed somewhere. I actually have no idea what happens to the dead bodies. I don't want to know.

Nobody around me acts surprised. It's better not to take much notice. And no one finds it very odd anymore. It makes grim sense. More and more people have been screaming volleys of words at the Speaking Bees and getting shot. It is a quick way out. And it is something I dream about. I imagine having the chance to shout again…to scream…even to just sing softly. As I look at the large body being carted away I realize that I envy the man. In my dreams now, I picture myself speaking. Shouting. Singing. In one dream I'm talking out loud with my parents. No masks. We're saying whatever we want. It seems like paradise. And then I wake up and feel the heat around me and realize again, for the thousandth time, that the world of my dreams is no more. Instead I'm alone in my bed with a mask, trying to breathe slowly.

After the large man's body is cleared from the stage, the loudspeaker gives off three rhythmic beeps followed by the standard pre-recorded sanitary announcement which is used anytime there is a security issue. The soothing voice of Mrs. Manners says, "Please remember: indoor voices and kind words."

A young lady who is next steps forward. She lifts her filter and speaks her word softly into the microphone, "Laughing." The audience clapped quietly. The young lady replaces her mask and exits the stage.

***

Mrs. Manners was used for everything: important announcements, daily reminders, bedtime routines. Every evening when people received their miracle poison pills it was Mrs. Manners who chimed in, encouraging us to swallow the pills quickly. Mrs. Manners told us the pills were medicine, but I know they're not. I don't know what they are, but they aren't medicine. I think they are for regulation. They seemed to slow everything down. The pills and the predictable repetition of the announcements and reminders helped crowd-control. During pill-taking time Mrs. Manners would recite phrases like a kind of mantra. She said things like: "Walk. Don't run." "Take deep, slow breaths." "Swallow all your pills." "Love your planet."

When my parents were still here, the only time I felt free from the system all around me was at night. Late at night, after the last Mrs. Manners announcements, mother used to creep out of her bed and sit next to me to read softly to me from her book. It was mother's calm reading which helped me settle into a comfortable breathing pattern for sleep. As she read the book I felt a comfortable silence settle around me.

The book spoke about a different world. It told stories about that world in magical ways.

The more and more mother read to me, the more I felt the truth that what was happening around me in the hot air and in the stifling moments beneath the masks was inevitable. It had happened before. It was happening now. Even in other worlds the foundations seemed to crack. Even in other galaxies there was no future complete shining and bright.

Last month, before my parents were transferred, mother gave the book to me. She said it was mine now. I started reading it to myself every night. Lately I have been carrying it around with me because it reminds me of her.

Last night I read long into the night. I found a new story in the book that I had never read before. In the story there was another city. This city was ruled by a great king. He had complete control over all information in the land. In the story there was a special queen who was very beautiful. She was one of many queens, but the king seemed to like her best. Everything she did pleased him.

The queen was 13, like me. Also like me the queen wasn't allowed to speak to the king unless she was given permission. If she wanted to speak she had to take a chance. She could show up in his throne room and hope he was in a good mood. Otherwise he might condemn her to death.

One day the queen realized her people were going to be destroyed by an evil court sorcerer. The sorcerer told lies. He desired to lead the people of the city astray. He was filled with malicious information of every kind. He wanted to destroy the people of the queen's family. She needed to get the king's attention in order to prevent the slaughter. But that meant she had to take a chance. The queen wasn't sure what to do, but then a friend told her something which clarified her mind. The friend said, "Who knows whether you have not come to the kingdom for such a time as this?"

The queen decided. She came before the king. He decided to let her speak. She said that she wanted to prepare a special meal for the king and for the sorcerer. The king agreed to her request.

The queen prepared wonderful food, and as the king and the sorcerer ate they eventually became full and happy. And then, the queen spoke.

She said, "If I have found favor in your sight, O king, and if it please the king, let my life be granted me for my wish, and my people for my request. For we have been sold, I and my people, to be destroyed, to be killed, and to be annihilated. If we had been sold merely as slaves, men and women, I would have been silent, but we are meant to be slaughtered."

Then the king said to the queen, "Who is he, and where is he, who has dared to do this?"

And the queen said, "A foe and enemy! This wicked sorceror! It is he who distorts the air. It is he who tells the lies. It is he who confuses the ears of the soldiers and tries to make them kill my people ruthlessly."

The king was so angry he walked to the nearest balcony to breath some fresh air to calm himself. The sorcerer, in fear for his life, begged the queen to do anything she could to spare him. As he begged her he tripped and fell on the hem of her dress. When the king came back he saw the sorcerer on the queen's hem and believed that the sorcerer was trying to assault the queen. He roared and commanded the sorcerer be hung from the gallows.

I looked up from reading the story in the book. I held a single page and it quivered between my fingers. I thought about the special queen and her world of silence. I thought about her brave voice. I thought about the hateful speech of the sorcerer. Then I put the book back beneath my pillow and slowly, in the pressing heat around me, I fell into a fitful sleep.

That night, I had a dream.

In my dream, I saw my parents. I saw my mother bending over to kiss me goodbye. In my dream, it's the day they left me. It's the day when they began their transfer journey north. I saw where they had been taken. They joined with a long line of other adults. All these parents had bent to kiss their children goodbye and then they began to walk along a thin path which wound through the forests into the north. The government had positioned guards along a route which led on and on into the distant reaches of the land.

The road stretched onward and my parents talked, whispered, with the people around them. "Where are they taking us?" they asked. No one knew. They exchanged stories of what the old world was like. They each remembered snatches of moments from before the earth turned hot and untouchable far south. There had been fragrant springs and summer beaches. There was rain and sometimes snow. The parents talked about how they might imagine a new world for their children. Might it be possible for things to heal, they wondered? Could the future be bright for their sons and daughters?

The road wound on and on. And then, in the distance, there was a sound. It was a sound unlike anything anyone had heard before. It was tremendous and guttural. It was as though the earth itself was heaving, far below the surface, and the sound was the manifestation of a deep, churning mark of scornful accusation...against humanity, against the scrambling people who hid and peeped about in masks for fear of the avenging wave of cleansing heat slowly wiping its way across the planet like a razor blade.

The road crested a small rise, and there, far below, was the source of the sound. It was a factory. It was absolutely massive. It was black-walled and scorched from within by some yet unseen and unimaginable horror. A sound from the factory rose high in the thin air. It was the sound of a deep scream, metallic and whining, like tortured gears. It was a sharp sound that carried upon it visions of digestion and intestinal turbulence. Inside the walls, the factory worked ceaselessly. Pistons and gears turned and shuddered in the hulking shadows of massive pillars which reached into the sky. Tubes and pipes from the factory looped outward to plunge down, deep into the earth below. They pulsed and writhed and pumped a thick, slow-moving sludge through their portals and avenues into the depths of the earth. The factory seemed to shimmer with a haze of industry and heat-filled, insect-like movement and frittering. It moved as though it was alive.

In my dream I saw my parents move forward as the line of people continued downward into the vast plain before the factory. The people were marched slowly across the eternal, flat ground, and, with each step, the factory grew in front of them until it contained and sapped all vision within itself. It was too large to be grasped. It was the most tremendous and hulking structure ever built. Looking upon it caused one's vision to buckle against the impossibility of its immensity. It stretched from end to end to a width of thousands of thousands of miles. It's towering levels of black stone and steel reached into the sky, dwarfing the plain beneath it. It was so high that clouds drifted in and out of the angled spires and antennas at its uppermost reaches. Lightning flashed from the dark sky and caught itself on the tips of the structures as though it were mere flashes of tinsel.

A huge door opened in the side of the walled factory, a door big enough to swallow a hundred tanker ships, and when the door reached its outermost angle, a deafening boom sounded across the plain, echoing into the heavens. The line of people moved forward and into the bowels of the factory. Their faces were bent forward as though they were hypnotized by the impossible girth which stretched before them. My parents' eyes became glazed and dark, unblinking beneath heavy lids. Their mouths slackened until they drooped open, lifeless and limp, trembling slightly with each step they took. And then, the door slowly creaked shut. As it did, I knew something about that moment. I could feel it in my dream. The people within would never return to the sunlit lands.

I saw then, in my dream, in some impossible way, through some unimaginable vision, what was truly happening to the people who were taken north. I saw what plan had been unfolding ever since the beginning of our masked lives. Ever since the dawn of this new terrible age of heat and oppressive crowding in the tiny winding halls of the Speaking Bees. I understood why no one ever returned from their transfers to the north. The factory of the north was a continent-spanning atmospheric processor. It ringed the upper dome of the earth as though it were a sick cap atop a fevered head. Its turning bowels administered planetary shots of medicine directly into the subterranean arteries of the deeply poisoned earth's central nervous system. The factory was there to monstrously and uncontrovertibly heal the earth and return it to a state of rebirth in some perversely imagined future possibility of redemption and karmaic, fever-seething fantasy.

I saw, in my dream, the government officials, nervously worrying over their ever-dwindling space on the planet. I saw them puzzling over past patterns of human behavior. I watched them calculate what might be necessary to return the earth to some past state of calm reprieve. I heard them whispering about hopes for a future government, free from the conflicting stresses of fossil fuels and refined oil. I saw them realize what the earth would require was a sacrifice. The altar of the planet's birth cradle required a sacrifice too great to comprehend yet too urgent to deny. The sins of the fathers must be visited upon the children for generations upon generations until the entire mad crawl toward progress which began sometime in centuries past could finally be fully held within the hands of the future and reckoned wanting. The cure the planet needed must come from the germ which had caused the disease. The earth needed to be fed with the healing circulatory power of the human animal. For the world to live, those who crawled upon its surface and drank for eons from its troughs would need to give fully of themselves to replenish the vast stores of tectonic growth stored far below.

In my dream I saw each sacrificed human being funneled forward into a vast, gaping hole at the factory's center. The terror of the moment rendered each one of them speechless and dumb before their awaited moment of sacrifice. Each person was stripped of their outer garments, entering the planet's crust as they came into the world, naked and unprotected. Each person was delivered forward into the maw where their body then fell, impossibly far, down and down, through and past rock and magma, seared and torched from below and above and all sides, by the angry fires of the planet's beating heart.

And there, within the center of the floating earth, each person fed a slowly building pool of healing, blood-fueled ointment at the center of the earth which was being cooked and simmered until the conditions were just right. And from that pool of human offerings, from that subterranean bowl of the intermingling of human and planetary unity, someday, when the conditions were right, a new world would be born.

I awoke from my dream and could barely stop myself from screaming.

***

After the nightmare I sat awake in my bed as the morning slowly dawned around me. I understood it now. I saw where our huddled lives were leading. I comprehended the slow, dumbing effect of the matron minders and their rules and the pills upon pills with their deadening, head-filling effect. There was a future. There would be a cosmic rebirth. And we were all the collective spark which would light it deep within the planet's core.

As I was leaving my room to come here to the Speaking Bee today the last thing I did was to grab my mother's book. I was nervous this morning, wondering what I would say when it was my turn. But, I've had some time to think. I've played the scenes and memories back in my head. In my mind, I've kissed my parents goodbye. I'm picturing their smiling faces right now. I choose to see their faces alive and smiling rather than the slack, sallow way they must have looked when they entered the factory maw so far in the northern lands. That's how I want to remember them, during their last few moments on earth.

It's now my turn in line. I step forward. The crowd in front of me is enormous. I can't see the back of the auditorium. I hear the collective sound of the hissing, ventilated breathing made by thousands and thousands of masks at once.

I hold the book into the air above my head. For a moment I close my eyes and picture green meadows, deep valleys, snow, and banquets of real food. I imagine my mother reading me stories from the book. I see the city on a mountain reaching up to the heavens with its crowds of people. I see the waters raging across the surface of the earth in that other world. I picture the silent queen standing in front of the king, waiting for her moment to speak. I see a chosen boy, standing above the world, bringing a voice of calm silence to the masses below.

I open my eyes and lift my filter. I open the book in my hands. I see my path forward. I will realize my own rebirth. I will have it forced upon me by no one. I see a way to return me to the beginning. I will shout out the incantatory words.

I see the guards reacting from the sides of the stage as they realize what is about to happen. Without realizing it, I smile. The first real smile I've had in heaven knows how long. I shout at the top of my lungs. It feels absolutely wonderful. I shout, *"In the beginning God created the heavens and the earth!"*

Acknowledgements

These stories have previously appeared in the following places.

"Their Foot Shall Slide in Due Time" D&T Publishing

"The Beast in the Hollow" Long Con Fiction

"Alice and Roses" Zoetic Press

"The Programmed Joy of Protection" House of Zolo

"Lidérc" 7th Circle Pyrite

"One Particular Girl On a Stage" ELJ Publications

The following stories originally appeared in a shorter format in the following places:

"Ramla Realizes" as "My Birth God is Anubis" Wolfsinger Publications

"Strawberry Skin" as "Strawberries" Worm Moon

A note about "The Beast In the Hollow"

Mihály Munkácsy is one of the most famous Hungarian artists. The three paintings of Christ referred to in this piece are real. Otherwise Munkácsy's life and death as depicted in this piece is entirely invented for the purposes of the story.

About the Author

Zary Fekete grew up in Hungary. He has a debut novella (*Words on the Page*) out with DarkWinter Lit Press and a short story collection (*To Accept the Things I Cannot Change: Writing My Way Out of Addiction*) out with Creative Texts. He enjoys books, podcasts, and many many many films. Twitter and Instagram: @ZaryFekete